THE LOTUS CREW

STEWART MEYER'S
THE LOTUS CREW

MIDNIGHT
CLASSICS

LONDON / NEW YORK

Library of Congress Catalog Card Number: 95–71067

First published in 1984 by Grove Press Inc, New York

Copyright © 1984 by Stewart Meyer

The right of Stewart Meyer to be identified as the author of this
work has been asserted by him in accordance with the Copyright,
Designs and Patents Act 1988

This edition first published in 1996 by Serpent's Tail, 4 Blackstock
Mews, London N4, and
180 Varick Street, 10th floor, New York, NY 10014

Cover design by Rex Ray
Printed in Great Britain by Cox & Wyman Ltd, Reading, Berkshire

To Jenny

. . . and a pinch of powder
to the wind for Somnus, the
Father of Sleep.

I wish to acknowledge my parents, for the first breath;
Bill Burroughs, who "scratched the surface," and the
following friends whose faith sustained me:
Howard Brookner, Roy Burman & Giselle, Ann Moradfar,
Jacques Stern, Herbert Huncke, James Grauerholz, John
Giorno, Dr. Joseph Gross, Lance Spano, and Harris Glasser.

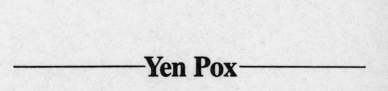

Yen Pox

". . . Trust not in the multitudes.

They are always wrong . . ."

Walk the Plank

They can smell yen* on a Caucasian. Both vendadors and police have a sixth sense for it and know you're out of synch, tense, anxious about essentials. You are down on Earth with one thought: to keep it brief. You don't care how overt your obsessiveness becomes to Earthlings. Puny exploited sacks of shit and pus. How could they understand anything?

Delancey Street crackled shameless like a neon leper colony. It was a dismal October afternoon in the year 1982. A cold mist abstracted *the street*.

Alvira's eyes periscoped over the rim of his gray sunglasses, and he took in the social order of the park like a demented anthropologist. No need to approach anyone. The monkey would take care of it.

"Señor, the Toilet is open. Open an' smokin', poppa. Yus' sit on thee bench an' hab j'muny ready." Moving with metronomically correct loose-skeleton boogie-bebob gestures, the touter attempted to usher Alvira over to the bench

---

*A glossary of street terms is provided on page 146.

where Toilet was operating, extending a wiry Latin arm with tracks along the main vein.

Alvira saw the three-man crew; one guy fanning bags, one taking cake, another looking mean. An evolving population of mostly blanco junkies waited impatiently to get near the bagman for their play and haul ass away from the muggers and cops who make their daily bread tormenting lotus users. Of course, being heat on junk turf is no breeze. Nobody backs down. A slumbum will not drop his dick in public. If he does he can't pick it up.

"Lookin' for Black Sunday, B. You see'm around?"

"Sunday close. Cops take their bags. On'y got Toilet, poppa. On'a muny On'a muny." The touter drew the fingers of his left hand together, kissed the tips, blew the kiss to God for creating such baaad shit. "No'sing touch Toilet out here, m'man. It's a monster. Be suckin' j'toes on uno bag."

"Thanks, man, I'll pass and take a walk. If I don't see Black Sunday I'll be back."

The thin lines of his conquistador moustache parted like a Venus's-flytrap as he smiled. "Buy dummies f'sho' go down that way." He pointed towards Rivington Street, across the park.

So that's where they were! Handy Carbona had told Alvira that the Sunday crew had no set spot but moved around the area from Houston Street to Forsyth, from Chrystie Street Park to Allen Street. Their boss was a blue-eyed Puerto Rican named Kono, who was the only one you could safely hand money to.

"Ba hondo!"

"Fao! Fao!"

"Agua! Ba hondo!"

They both turned as the cry spread through the park. Best not to make any sudden moves. Alvira walked slowly away from the touter and sat on a far bench. The Tactical prowler stood ten feet from the bench where Toilet had been operating. Customers and vendadors acting nonchalant, preoccupied, fooling no one. The moments crept by. They should all whip out Bibles and go into theopathic convulsions, Alvira thought. All you have to do with cops is be comprehensible.

"Red light! Keep walkin'!"

Alvira lit a cigarette and watched with mounting impatience, eyes watery, skin crawling. The sweat under his arms felt like harsh acid, lungs tight as if from a severe flu. If he didn't score soon he'd be farting butterscotch.

Two uniforms emerged from the prowler and began to hassle the Toilet crew. It's protocol to stash all bags when the lookouts cry out, so everyone was clean. But the cops were going to do their paper shit, their "warrant check," just to tie up the festivities. They did not appear to notice Alvira. He got up and walked slowly away from the bad news.

Might as well check Rivington Street. Sure enough, as he neared the bodega another touter smelled his yen.

"Black Sunday! Inside, secon' floor," the man said.

Alvira passed and went into the bodega, bought a container of coffee. He'd heard Sunday worked outside, not in buildings. He'd also heard people passed Black Sunday dummies. Only buy from Kono. Alvira watched for a few minutes. Business was thriving. Must be the real thing.

The touter gave him a strange look but stepped aside. A thick honcho inside was not as polite.

"Got tracks, m'man?"

"No tracks," Alvira said. "I sniff."

The man smirked. "No good, B. J'bad company." The honcho lifted his arm to signal for assistance, and Alvira saw another man move to surround him. "Spleet now, dig?"

"Wait, m'man, listen. Handy Carbona told me to look for Kono and score Sunday if I want to get straight. I used to score from Dr. Nova in this building, but I been away. You know Carbona?"

The honcho grinned. "Dude was on m'program. Gulp mo' Jesus jizz than any ten men." He called off his backup. "Why'nt j'say Handy sent j'? Go up. Hab j'muny ready."

Alvira walked farther into the shadowy abandoned building. Another crew worker sat on the stairs with a shotgun resting across his fat lap. He was talking to a wiry blood. "Blancos ain't no good on musical instruments, man. They should stick to calculators and typewriters." He looked up at Alvira. "Secon' floor on the left."

On the way up, it hit Alvira that something wasn't right. Just as vendadors and la hara smell yen, the junkie smells a ripoff or bust. Not the scents he was getting. Something, some small detail, was off. Alvira's left hand moved into his jacket pocket, where he slid the safety off his Raven .25 automatic. There was a round in the chamber. Whatever was off he'd cool.

On the second floor he scored without a hitch, giving two fifties to the cake taker and standing patiently, palm up, eyes down, as the bundle was metered out. Each bag was machine-tucked glassine stamped with the Black Sunday logo and shrink-sealed in plastic. According to Handy it was the only down bag on the street at the moment. Handy didn't schmooz anymore, but being the oldest wisest hippest junkie at the methadone program subjected him to endless sound whether he wanted it or not. The street yentas kept him up on what bag was smokin' at any given moment.

It was only as Alvira was on his way down the stairs with his bags that he realized what was wrong.

"Hold it, B," a crew worker said. "Cain't go out that way. Too hot. Too much in an' out." He jerked his head in the direction of the roof. "Go up to the top an' cross over to the nex' building. Let you out on Chrystie."

That was it. Dozens of people going in and nobody coming out.

Alvira nodded at the lookout as he made the roof. "How do I split?"

The Latin pointed to a plank of semirotten wood, maybe sixteen inches wide, stretching twelve feet between the building they were on and the next. "Walk the plank."

"What?"

Two blancos appeared, walked around the baffled Alvira,

12

and casually walked the plank. The wood bent and squeaked. The lookout shrugged.

Alvira looked down. A six-story drop onto concrete and broken glass. His legs vibrated with yen tension, palms sweaty, head swimming.

"C'mon. Take the stairs down to the open window an' pass into the nex' building. Let you out on Chrystie. On'y way, m'man, so make eet."

"Hmmmmmm, lemme just sit here'n hoof a bag so'm not jumpin' out of m'skin for this."

The lookout was amused. "Hey, if the man was on his way up here j'd be over that plank in a flash. Bu awri', B. Be quick."

Alvira slit a bag and sniffed powder off the tip of his blade. It was beige, even consistency, flat taste. Very strong. He lit a cigarette and looked up at an angry gray and crimson sky. Without further elaboration he took a deep breath and walked the plank. It trembled under his sneakers, but before he could register terror it was all over. He took the stairs down to the open window, made the next building, walked out on Chrystie Street.

Whew! What a body won't do for a religious experience.

"Gimmicks! Need a gimmick, poppa?"

He turned to face a light-skinned young Latin girl with jet-black lotus eyes, the skin pulled tightly over her face so you could see the bones.

"No gimmicks. Shit, you ever walk that plank?"

"Ebery day."

"They ever lose anyone on that number?"

"Not today. They gotta do it that way. Bery hot. Cops look for Sunday. Wan' a place to get off?"

Alvira didn't shoot and was staying just a block away with some friends. But he was in the mood to linger awhile in Lotus Land. After the eternal 'burbs of L.A. it was refreshing.

13

The girl led him to a cellar social club on Eldridge Street. He gave her five bucks and half a bag, then gutted and snorted two more off the tip of his blade. He looked around. Needles, blood, spoons, bottle caps, alcohol burners. A radio might have helped, but nothing frivolous would be appropriate. Just sounds of pain and pleasure punctuating the eternal jabber of a slumbum happy hour. Alvira was the only sniffer, the only square in the shooting gallery.

Momentarily he felt intense relief. Lungs loosened, nose and eyes stopped running, bones relaxed under the skin. He tapped a Three Castles cigarette out of a fresh pack and put the tip loosely between his lips. Alvira smoked moderately, and only pale fine Virginia.

"Hey, m'man, hit ch'jugular fi' bucks."

Alvira looked up at a tall thin black man with piss-yellow eyes and the broken face of an old prizefighter.

"Three if you got cho' own weeper."

"No thanks, m'fine."

"The man's fine by design," the black man said, "but watch yo' behin'."

Alvira smiled and looked away. Time to split. He usually liked to sit very still after fixing, but this was not the place. In retrospect walking the plank seemed trivial. His mind drifted back to L.A. He'd gone to clean up and stayed away from the goodness even though there was no shortage of brown Mex. But a few days before leaving for New York, he met a Chicano girl who liked to screw and suck up El Pico laced with opium and honey. After three weeks with Mr. Clean, relapse was like a ticket home. Alvira felt like your proverbial incongruity when not opiated. The physical and mental anguishes of withdrawal were perfectly tolerable. Being an Earthling was not. So time and again he went back to meet the monkey. Alvira and the Chinaman ate off the same plate.

*

Alvira left the club and walked over to Prince Street. He was staying for the time being in the loft of his friend Specs.

Specs was an old friend, from boyhood chalk on the factory wall, from afternoon sniffs in the school yard. "A pinch of powder to the wind for the souls who slip over into Endless Nod." Specs was a photographer and spent hours each day absorbed in quiet conception. QT, the dark-eyed girl who lived with him, silently hand-tinted Specs' photos. They were building a collection of character studies called *Inebriates* and were both so self-absorbed Alvira fit right in. There was something impalpable about his hosts that comforted him. When he got upstairs he found the inseparable pair sitting at a wide table sorting slides. Alvira dropped three bags before Specs.

"For you."

Specs looked up. "Hey, you don't have to do that. It doesn't cost us anything to have you stay here until you get settled."

"Don't be too generous, Alvira. You're going to need those bags," QT said.

"I'm fine. Got enough to hold me. T should hit town tomorrow evening, and then I'm set up. So please enjoy'm."

Specs didn't need to have his arm twisted too far back. He was not a junkie . . . heavens, no! His flair for decorous verbiage led him to the phrase "lotus enthusiast." It was something he did only occasionally, and never two days in a row. Specs carefully slit the bags open and tapped powder onto a hand mirror. Attention quietly focused as they sat around the tray for the healing ceremony, staring at thick snowy lines of goodness. Sniff! A 'shish pipe was lit to facilitate inebriation. The silence took on a harmonic divinity.

"So this is Black Sunday," Specs said, eyes reduced to sparkling slits. "It's better than Dr. Nova. Old Handy Carbona knows exactly of what he speaks."

"Yeah, it's gooood," Alvira said. "But wait until you get a take on T's pebbles. This material has to be stepped on a few times for safety. Easy to o.d. with, man. He gets'm straight from the Ayatollah—"

"Pebbles?"

"Yeah, and not reconstituted. The real thing. Light yellowish-beige, granulates coarse but breaks up quick in water. No quinine, nothing bitter. Burns to a clear amber drip."

"So what's he want from you, Alvira?"

"Well, you remember a few years back when T was putting out bags and I was working for him—"

"Yeah, before he dumped a few kilos of number four on that undercover jerk and went away."

"Right. One of life's embarrassing moments, for sure. He was released from prison a few months ago and went upstate to chill out. Muggles handles the reefer trade for him. He's covered. He just sits on his old wooden verandah and dreams up new mischief. Got a scheme for me to hear."

"Tommy always did incorporate you into his schemes."

"Only the wilder ones. Last time he was gonna form the Rainbow Society, sort of a crew based loosely on the Chinese Triads. Quite a historian, Tommy is. Obsessive about secret societies. Reads everything he can get his hands on, raps to people who know the score."

"So he's going to give it another shot?"

"Near as I can tell he got his uncle to spring for the seed cake, and his importer gave'm a nice low price for kilos."

"All he needs is a crew."

"Yeah, a Rainbow crew. All different nationalities."

"That's where you come in."

"I guess."

"Gonna do it, Alvira?"

Alvira shrugged. "I'm broke. The trip to L.A. tapped me out, and I've still got m'monkey. Got to do it. I just want to get by without the scuffle."

"And Tommy? What about him? He don't need money."

"Oh, Tommy—man, you know. He just wants to be the Emperor."

Child of Nova

John Jacob Pennington, age sixteen, had basic universal knowledge down to two self-evident premises. First: high school is a stone drag. Small wonder so many educated people committed suicide. Second: one thing made it tolerable. The goodness. With a little powdered cool he could calmly sit right through the most tedious pedantic fits his teachers could invoke. He didn't have to doodle or move his legs furiously back and forth or in any way tip his mitt to the fact that he was bored beyond reason by the asinine assumptions, the condescending smuggery, of his learned instructors. JJ's mind absorbed basic paradox gracefully. He knew that nobody really knows anything. Was that a secret? Had somebody forgotten to tell them? The teachers reminded JJ of ex-cons in that there was a dreary institutional predictability to them. Every ex-con he knew preconceived the same things in similar ways; stock questions and stock answers. Teachers were a notch below, actually. They were so busy cross-referencing and analyzing that they missed what was happening right under their noses.

JJ scratched his crotch and flipped pages of the book he

was reading. It was study-hall period, and he'd just administered a healthy bang of Dr. Nova in a deserted balcony above the auditorium. Now he'd be able to sit it out. Study-hall was one of the few periods JJ liked. It allowed him to read what he wanted. First he'd burned down various histories of Hannibal. Baddest warrior the world has ever seen, and dark like JJ. But history couldn't hold him. Who really knows what happened back then? People can't agree on what happened five minutes ago right in front of their faces.

The next phase of his reading career began with that cantankerous and kinky Englishman, the Beast. Crowley! The book was called *Diary of a Drug Fiend*, a title hard to resist. So, sitting in Martin Luther King Jr. Memorial Park on the corner of Dumont Avenue and Miller in East New York, JJ exposed himself to genteel blanco bohemianisms. "Prudence, I have some lovely heroin you *might* enjoy." Sheee-a-zit, Jim! It boggle the mind. JJ told Furman Whittle about Crowley, and a new regime kicked in. Drug literature. Together they braved dusty bloodless corridors of those bone-dry pavilions of illiteracy: libraries, most of them on college campuses, as what they were seeking had an air of contraband. This was their discovery after asking a maternal librarian for a copy of *Confessions of an English Opium-Eater* by De Quincey and receiving instead a verbose lecture that she didn't want mistaken for a verbal reprimand but, given her tact, had all the qualities of one. Evoking such passionate outpourings from so contained a creature further ignited their hungry young appetites.

Down in the coal room under JJ's building, where they hung out like the Mighty Mezz cloistered away from all those petty Earthlings up there, they started to build their own book collection. A slumbum Library of the Damned. Crowley, De Quincey, Baudelaire, Cocteau, Coleridge. Getting weary of the antique, they slid into Alexander Trocchi, Leroy Street, Piri Thomas, Malcolm X. They almost gagged on Burroughs but got it down. Burroughs was good to chill out on. Just like Billie Holiday was good to nod out on. A thick stolen *Webster's* dictionary cleared up the mysteries of words. Without the slightest effort their reading vocabularies were becoming immense. They could pull up some erudite verbiage and baffle Mr. Fob to the bone.

JJ was snapped out of his study hall dream-reading session by a sharp, obtrusive voice. A subtle bark, if there is such a thing.

"Reading Coleridge, are you, John Jacob?"

Lazy eyes looked up into the face of none other than Mr. Fob, a stiff disciplinarian and renowned imposer of sophomore English. JJ had recently concluded it was not the material that was dead but the delivery boy.

"Yesssa," JJ let out, perched over a copy of *Kubla Khan*, propping the lids open.

"You look very tired, John Jacob. Are you getting enough sleep these days?"

"Yesssa."

"Well, see that you're alert for *my* class. You are among my brighter students, and I expect your performance to reflect that fact. Say, are you high on something?"

"Nooooosssa!"

Mr. Fob did not look convinced. "John Jacob, if you allow yourself to use narcotics, you will be betraying the natural gifts God gave you. No one on drugs ever amounted to anything. You're not sheltered. You should know that."

"Yessssa." Shit, good thing Mr. Fob hadn't laid his sound on Coleridge, or there'd be no *Kubla Khan*.

Mr. Fob sat down, making his bulky form ridiculous by squeezing it into the undersized seat. "Please roll up your sleeves for me, John Jacob," he barked softly, eyes knowing and smug. He wrinkled his face like a jewel appraiser. "I've seen needle marks. If you have none I'll apologize, but—"

"Yesssssa." JJ, eyes painfully wide open, rolled up both sleeves of his cotton pastel-blue shirt. The arms were spanking clean, and he turned them over slowly so Mr. Fob could verify this. JJ never hit his arms. Like wearing a sign for the heat. As juicy as those lines were, he let them be.

"Well, they look clean to me," Mr. Fob said astutely, eyes straining through Coke-bottle wire rims. "But that doesn't mean you haven't taken pills or drunk something."

"Noooosssa. Jus' no sleep las' ni'. I was playin' basketball an' the guys aks me t' hang out'n sing late. We was hittin' fows an' bows all ni', sa. Dass all."

"Well, all right. Your eyes say something else, but I'll give you the benefit of the doubt. Say, are you in the glee club?"

"Ohh, noooossa. I c'n on'y sing fows an' bows wi' m'frien's. I don' likes t'be singin' nothin' else."

Mr. Fob's exasperated sigh marked the end of the conversation. He rose to his feet, shook his head, and went on to educate someone else.

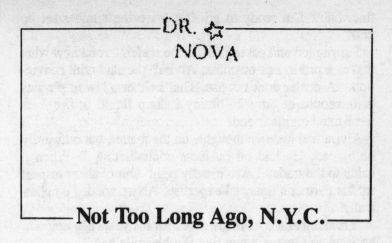

DR. ✩ NOVA

Not Too Long Ago, N.Y.C.

T lit a thick reefer of golden-red Jamaican and looked out the window at a perpetually teeming Sheridan Square. He hadn't been out of the joint long enough to adjust to having so many options and didn't know what to do first. He was about to throw on his jacket and take a walk when the buzzer sounded. That was rare. The bell plate downstairs was a dummy. In order to ring you had to remove the plate and connect two wires underneath. It was either Alvira or one of the Rastas bringing him some cake from the ganja shops. Praise Jah. He glanced at a mirror that afforded full view of the front stoop. It was Alvira.

T clicked into his business personality as he buzzed the door open. Mr. Sparks waited for footsteps on the stairs.

"Alvira, I thought you stepped out of the circle, m'man. You're two days late."

"Yeah, I had a little blowout while you were gone, T. Figured I committed myself to being a good boy once we start, so I'd party one last time for—"

"You have a habit?"

"Naw. Didn't run that long. Just three or four days. I feel

fine, baby. I'm ready to go. You have the number set up yet?"

T shrugged and passed Alvira the reefer. "You know what makes a pro in this business, Alvira?" he said with conviction. "A dealer does not use. That's either a law of physics or it should be, dig?" Tommy's sharp liquid brown eyes were fixed on his friend.

Alvira had his own thoughts on the matter, but outwardly he agreed. He had no business contradicting T. When it came to the trade, T was usually right. Out of sheer respect for his partner's financial expertise, Alvira nodded emphatically.

"I remember a cool that worked for me years ago uptown, back when I was running that Doublesmile bag."

"Yeah, before you went to the can. That had to be three years ago."

"Yeah. So this cool would meet me once a week, and I'd pass him the medicine all bagged and ready. Fifties, with the Doublesmile logo stamped on each sealed quarter-gram bag. He'd hand me the cake from the last bunch, and I'd hand him the new material. I never once counted the cake, Alvira. It was always on the money. This was cookin' for maybe six months. The two of us were splitting over four grand weekly behind this number, so I just assumed I was the best friend this cool ever had and he'd never fuck me over, you know? So one day I show and he's got the shorts. Some riff about his wife's sick and he dropped two grand on specialists. But while he's talkin' I can sense his condition. I figured he just had a little blowout like the one you're talkin' about . . . "

Alvira flushed.

" . . . So I told him we'd split the shorts and handed him his next week's material as if everything was natch. I never saw him next week, Alvira. Never seen him since. Imagine blowin' that kind of weekly turn for a lousy burn."

"Pretty shortsighted," Alvira conceded.

"Fuckin' stupid is what it is. But when a man's usin' he's

not there anymore. You ask him a question and Jones answers for him. Tell him to expel Jones and he says, 'What Jones?' I been in the game too long for that sound, Alvira. I don't want to hear it from anyone. Certainly not a friend."

Alvira's eyes tightened. "If you're worrying about me, T, I'm steppin' out of the box. I know myself. If I say I'm gonna do it right, that's what'll happen. I didn't try'n hide my blowout, and I didn't do it on credit." Alvira looked towards the door. "If I'm going to worry you let's chill it out right now—"

T put his open palm up in a bid for silence. "Don't talk like that, Alvira. I set this up for the two of us, and that's the way the play stays. I trust you. That's rare on this planet, but I do. God knows why. Just an instinct I guess. If I'm soundin' down on you it's because I know our friend Mr. Jones too well. I don't want him workin' against us. You're gonna have to face some tasty schmooz in this game. Every time we re-up material we'll have to sample it. Extreme caution is in order or Jones will make his presence felt. Believe me."

"I hear you."

"This is a chance for us to take some real steps forward, Alvira. We'll triple our cake on the first play, and you'll get acquainted with my supply people so you can negotiate future buys without me. We'll be sittin' right if this goes down. Think about it."

"Oh, hey, I think about it all the time."

Alvira broke eye contact to fumble for a match. He lit a Three Castles and sat back, relieved that T had turned his attention to preparing another reefer.

A slight tremble passed through Alvira, and he recognized the modulation of his system from opiated to mild yen. A gentle hunger, not a fierce need. Another few days and he'd've found himself in trouble.

"Here, Alvira, this reefer's laced with freebase. Should distract you from the blowout blues."

Alvira sat back comfortably in a soft blue chair by the

window, dreaming about his first sniff in the school yard long ago. He'd felt better at once, as if some great abstract adjustment had been made. Boyhood chalk on the street for years. A lot of time had passed since he'd played handball on the factory wall, watching the workers perform their tediums through bleak dirt-smoked windows. Alvira swore he'd never end up like that. It'd be like doing time without a conviction.

"Alvira, you seem miles away. Dreamin' about all the cake you're gonna make?"

"Just dreamin', actually, about a pinch of powder to the wind on a gray afternoon years ago."

T knew the ritual. A pinch of powder to the wind for the souls who've slid into Endless Nod.

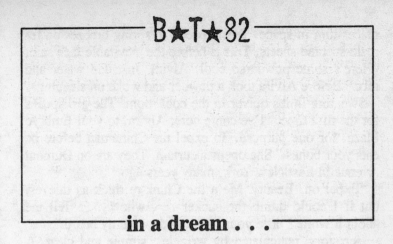

in a dream . . .

Alvira wipes the sediment of centuries off his clothes and steps into the girl's chambers. Bare blue walls, a small functional bed, and, beside it, a tiny night table with a green-shaded copper lamp. Unseen· radio plays rude-boy music in the distance. He lies on the bed with detached amusement, sinks into the comfort of sheets, female smells. Unfamiliar luxuries prevail. The girl is showering. Alvira sits and smokes a thick memory chip. The girl appears, a smooth graceful entity. Olive skin draped in a sparse towel. Dark eyes widen as he tears the towel off her cakes and pounces on the flesh cookies. Gobble gobble giggle giggle. Taste of girl dew as silver streaks appear on taut thighs.

Later he cradles the cool round balls of her ass and drifts off into lotus. First time in years he gets there without the powder. An energy coming through, dimly familiar but impossible to locate or trigger. Something from another lifetime. Before he was the Alvira Kid.

The dark-eyed girl is Beauty. A glinting twinkle of pleasure in her attention causes him to pulse with anticipation. She who looks at him and perceives the tradition of kin that places him in space. Tensions ebb to spring breezes on female-scented sheets. This is before the inevitable face said, "Here's some powdered cool, Alvira. Just add water and mix." Before Alvira took a powder and woke up sleeping.

Sweating limbs quiver in the cool room. The girl speaks for the first time. "I've come here, Alvira, to your Embryo Plaza, for one purpose. To expel the Chinaman before he eats your bones." She opens a curtain. They are on Dumont Avenue in East New York, many years ago.

"Expel on, Beauty. Me'n the Chink're thick as thieves, but if I could dump the sucker . . . whew. . . . Tell me about it while I taste your morning dew on my beard."

Her story, punctuated by wriggles, simple and clear. A drug dealer's daughter, she would come to be his heroin.

Eyes softly close. Her lips on his as sirens wail through arteries and conduits. Packs of wild dogs scurry through abandoned tenements. Smell of leather jackets and cheap wine in doorways. Distant blow-harmonies chime like voices playing tricks with the wind in the dismal alleyways and dank subway stations.

"Step inside me, Alvira."

Girl goodness upon his tongue, dance the tarantella through a cool crack of moonlight. A golden glow deep inside expels the Chinaman. The creature under him—fruit of some higher being's boredom—squirms gently under his weight.

Petty virtues and sobriety can't reach you here, Alvira. Step inside Beauty, where your solids turn to vapors.

BLACK MARK

Arteries and Conduits

They left T's Jaguar on Third Avenue in a nice neighborhood so it'd be there when they returned, and took a battered VW bug down to the street. It was Friday, a busy time, and twilight was filling out rich and blue. A mild temperature and lack of precipitation gave the night a crispness Alvira found comforting. Almost felt like nothing could go wrong under such ideal conditions. But he knew the feeling to be without substance. A misleading calm prevailed as they descended on Alphabet City. The biggest smack emporium on the East Coast stretched before them as they drove through narrow bombed-out streets. Blacks, Latins, blancos, shadows in somber colors; lips tight and drawn down, eyes dead but active with the scuffle. Waiting, watching, copping, splitting. Lots of verbs on the street.

"Alvira, you've heard of the Sun Belt, the Snow Belt. This here is the Dope Belt. We're going to cross above the main action, then ride Avenue D into the thick of it," T said, hands gripping the wheel. "We'll be pretty safe inside, but keep the windows up just in case. Anyone gets in front of

27

this car in a mean way is gonna have tire tracks across his forehead."

They passed rows of abandoned buildings thick with clusters of crew workers and customers. Hostile cautious eyes observed their every move. Blancos could only be doing one of three things here. Copping, getting mugged, or making arrests.

"I'm not worrying, T," Alvira said with lazy unconcern. He had complete confidence in T's ability to negotiate junk turf. Tommy's instincts on the street consisted of a finely tuned receiver system refined by years of practice. In the old days almost all his scoring buddies had been mugged a few times on these very streets. Some slid around easy, befriending a crew worker, staying cool, avoiding the cops and muggers. But some had been cut, beaten, robbed, even killed, over a few bags of dope. There were gangs that specialized in ripping off whites who came into the neighborhood for drugs, and that was the only reason they came, so it was safe for a thief to assume that any blanco who looked even vaguely like a junkie would either have money or bags in his possession.

That was only part of what was uncool about junk turf. The shooting galleries and scoring spots were in dingy apartments in abandoned buildings, set up so that you usually had to walk a few dark, crawling flights. Often someone was waiting in a corridor or apartment ready to tax the next pair of legs coming down the stairs. Nothing personal. Give up your dope or your life. Usually you scored on one flight and took off on another. Then if you were lucky you made it to the street again and got your ass out of there. If unlucky you might end up stuck in an apartment with your money, watch, wallet, shoes, coat, maybe even pants gone. Not to mention your medicine.

Years ago someone had tried to take Alvira off in a building on East Third Street. Alvira took a deep cut over his left eye before the sleazoid got an ice pick between the ribs for his effort. Alvira thought of finishing him off but took pity on the junk-sick slumbum as he lay squirming in his own blood. So he just kicked him in the face a few times, broke the fingers on his knife hand, and walked out of the building with the mugger's bags as well as his own. For years Alvira'd chastised himself for not wasting the sucker. A citizen has a duty to rid society of elements that prey on the innocent. Oh, well . . .

"Put that reefer out, Alvira!" T barked. "Our asses are on the line here. Aside from crooks and thieves we have to watch for the man. Rare they bother customers, but it happens. My parole officer would skin me for a pot pinch."

"I hear you," Alvira said, rolling down the window just enough to dump the reefer. "I left my smoke in the Jag, T. I'm clean now."

"Cool. Now here we are, so watch what happens."

T pulled up on the corner of Eighth Street and Avenue D. Immediately two boys in green shirts and blue jeans approached.

"Green Tape is on," one of them said. "How many?"

T slid the window down two inches. "Get us six bags of Green Tape, frien', but make sure the bags are stamped and sealed. I know a dummy when I see one."

The boy's eyes were pinned, reading them as he took the order and received the information that his customers were not new to the street and knew the score. He told them to wait a minute, then split into a basement ten feet away.

"They work this corner in crews, Alvira. The Green Tape boys wear green shirts or caps. The Black Mark boys wear black caps. Those are the two main ops. Others come and go. Dr. Nova also works here from time to time, but they're harder to spot. You have to know a face or go to their social club on Rivington Street where they're covered and more relaxed. Dr. Nova puts out a better bag, but Green Tape is easier to score."

"A year ago this corner belonged to LaTuna," Alvira reflected. "When you were in the can I scored here a few times."

"LaTuna is legendary lotus, Alvira. Best street bag in years. The crews that work this corner allow only bad competition. But LaTuna is around. Their headquarters is in Brooklyn, right over the Manhattan Bridge in a mostly Jamaican area. They're covered over there, and nobody fucks with them. Over here they catch shit. Their main op now is to move into an abandoned building, set up their steerers on the street, and do business up towards the roof for a few days before moving on. Their steady customers seem to find them. They leave a touter at the old spot to hip regulars to the new spot."

Alvira knew the wrinkle. You scan for a familiar face, and the face leads you home.

"Here comes our Green boy," Tommy said.

The runner bopped up to the driver's side, his right hand in a tight fist.

T let three crisp twenties slip through the vent window, but only after examining the stamp and seal on each bag. "Thanks, B," he said. "If we like these we'll be back."

"Aks f'René," the slumbum said. "I always be here. 'Member the name. René treat j'ri', poppa. These otha guys be passin' dummies ebery chance dey get. I gib j'goooood shit."

"I hear you, René."

"Take care, poppa. Enjoy j'medicine."

T slid René an extra five and closed the window. The VW pulled away from the hottest curb in lower Manhattan and took D straight down to East Houston.

"Now, Alvira, we're gonna give these bags to Joey Giggles for analysis. I wanna know what's sellin' out there, and being that we're the ones with the most to lose, the market research falls on our asses."

"Sounds cool."

"Say, notice how René looked at us. Checked us both good. He is in the business of remembering faces. Pop up in three weeks and he'll know you."

30

They drove back to the Jag, stashed the bags, went back to junk turf. "Next stop's an abandoned building on Third between B and C. This is LaTuna, for today at least. No telling where they'll open tomorrow. I hear they're putting out a very good bag these days, but it's not really the original people, so you never know. There're a multitude of tricks. Powdered barbiturates and Valium, injectable methadone. Just don't know what you're getting, even after you shoot it. Giggles will have to do a breakdown of the composition."

They parked around the corner from their destination. This scene was considerably more dangerous because they had to get out of the car and walk into a deserted building. One of the LaTuna guards recognized T, and they got in with no trouble.

"That guy knows my face from the joint."

Inside, a practiced crew kept traffic organized.

"LaTuna has the best communications system in Alphabet City," T said as they labored up the narrow, unlit, crumbly staircase. "Guys on the rooftops watching the man. Long before heat arrives the bagman's ditched his stash and may be whipping out a pack of cards or a Bible, or tryin' to beat it out of the building. Very hard to catch'm with the bags. It happens sometimes, but . . ."

The building was an old abandoned red-brick jumping with shadows. Steerers organized the flow of junkies with precision. A theater of ghosts.

"I don't like this, T. Wish I had my piece."

T had insisted Alvira leave his .25 automatic in the car. Alvira had the rep of being less than discreet when it came to pulling iron. T kept his own .22 strapped flat to his tight belly. A loose beige unconstructed jacket hid the print of the piece under his shirt.

"Just get the cake fanned out and make the buy, Alvira. Don't look hard at the bagman. Makes'm nervous. Act preoccupied with the bags he's counting out."

"Shouldn't be too hard."

They both engaged in a chilly laugh from another lifetime.

On the fourth floor another worker stood in the corridor, blocking the stairway. The thick young Latin eyed them suspiciously under a pulled-down navy watch cap, then pointed towards an apartment at the end of a dark passageway. The hall was lined with blanco customers standing one behind the other, pressed against the wall. Occasionally a few went into the apartment, and the line moved up. Then a few came out, obviously having scored, and more entered. Everything seemed rehearsed and perfected. Aside from the bagman inside the apartment, there was a worker at the door regulating traffic, and another walking the length of the line over and over, checking faces, saying, "Hab j'money ready. Fan it out face up. Hey, shuddup on line, I gotta hea' w'z goin' down. Dinero fanned out o' j'loose j'turn! Cop'n split! Don' run!"

Alvira fanned out tens like a poker hand. When it was their turn the door worker tried to break them up. "We're buyin' together, B," he told the man, slipping him a deuce.

"Cool."

The apartment windows were caked with dirt or lined with ripped paper. Two flickering candles provided the only light. As Alvira approached the bagman he became aware of another crew worker. The apartment had a foyer off the main room, and in it sat a huge honcho with what looked like an Uzi draped across his lap. The candles flickered, and soon all Alvira could see was the glow of the man's cigarette.

"Gimme six," Alvira said, passing the fanned-out bills to the bagman.

"Five! J'payin' f'five," the bagman said, almost looking up over the rim of his hat, catching himself before he made eye contact.

"Gimme six f'five, baby. Don't I get a play when I score half a bundle?"

The bagman's teeth glinted in the dark as he smirked at the dumb blanco. "Where you been, poppa? No mo' play no way. Buy nine hundred ninety-nine bags, I gib j'one free."

"Damn, you people used to give me a nice play back—"

"Nobody git no play. It's better shit. Cos' more t'operate. I yus' a workin' man, poppa. M'boss say *no play*. Now split. I gotta keep thee line movin'."

"Sure," Alvira said as he closed his fist around the half-bundle, turned, marched indignantly out the door.

There was a shooting gallery on the floor below, and on their way down someone asked if they wanted to get off. Three bucks if they had their own works. Otherwise six. It was a hard sell. The man said his friend inside could hit so professional there'd be no marks.

"O' how'z 'bout a jugular hit, m'man?"

"Thanks. We pass."

"You know, sometimes they raze one of these buildings and find corpses stuffed all over the fuckin' place," T said. "In the basements, apartments, just about anywhere."

"Makes sense. That jugular dude must make a fortune with skills like that."

"Alvira, this scene is too frantic for the likes of me, but this is where the *real* money is. I mean, you can set up as a house connection, and if you're lucky and establish the right clientele you'll sporadically make out. You know, middle-class customers always cleaning up on you when you're holding. But the street spells infinite demand and limited supply. It's nothing for a good crew to turn eighty grand a day. LaTuna is sold out before the sun goes down. They start the morning heavy and sell out before the noon drop. The afternoon stuff is gone by seven or eight."

"What about Green Tape?"

"Goes all night. Also Black Mark. Twenty-four hours of goodness. That whole corner is nonstop no matter what. If they run out of one there's the other. Run out of both, they just tell you to wait or walk around and come back. That's bad because customers accumulate and make the vendadors nervous. The heat knows what's happenin' when they see a swarm of floating blanco flotsam hanging around. So the crew workers don't like the wait any more than the customers. They try to facilitate fluid in-and-out traffic. If they're well organized there's an extra stashman to pick up the next batch while the bagman works what he's got. I know one of the bosses, a guy named Chu. He was just fired from La-Tuna. Chu's Dominican, and the Puerto Ricans in LaTuna gave him a hard time. He's the dude who's going to take us to the ShyWun. The crew leaders are supplied by the owners, who are supplied by the Cuban mobs and others. Lots of independents these days. Run it a week, get rich, cool out. Longer action requires connections. Chu knows a major player who's going to do us a lot of good. Not on the supply end. I have my uncle's people for that. But the ShyWun can see to it that we don't step on toes or draw excessive heat. Forget about us selling to existing crews. The cash in this business is in retail. What we need is protected space where we can run our crews. These brandname scores are run like conservative businesses; workers get a commission on a per-bag basis, except for touters and lookouts, who're on salary. Green Tape comes out of the basement our man René ran into on Eighth Street, although sometimes it shifts to a doorway, a van parked on the street. Sometimes you see the bagman sitting in a parked car in broad daylight feeding the runners as if he had a license. No one seems to notice. They rarely get busted, never ripped off."

"And Black Mark?"

"One of our people told me the Mark walks over in a baby carriage. Never the same girl pushin' it, and no idea with who or where it's dropped off. Seems to change. A tight ever-evolving system. Very complex; procedurally repetitive but confusingly unpredictable. Obviously the work of a highly developed criminal computer of some sort."

"Jumpin' Jesuits!" Alvira said. "Order one for me!"

34

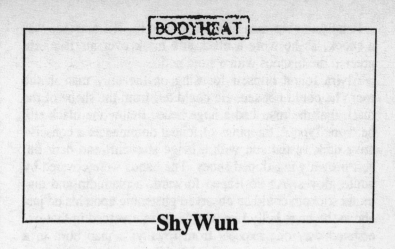

ShyWun

"The ShyWun don't go near *the street*, babies," Chu said, looking at his blanco associates with a smug sparkle. "Bu' I see wh' I c'n do."

The meet was made for that evening, in Hartford, Connecticut. T drove them out in the Jag, enjoying the erotic feeling of commanding the car's awesome weight and power with one finger and one toe.

Chu directed them to the cemetery, where a huge black van was waiting to take them to the ShyWun.

The van's smoked glass afforded no view, so when they were finally unloaded they had no idea where. A small private estate, thick hedges on all sides. A huge imposing wooden house with a wide verandah stood before them. It looked more like a sea-resort rooming house fallen from juicy times than a New England dwelling.

They were led into a large room lined with oak, and sat down near a coffee table piled with Remy, cocaine, reefers, and even coffee.

Chu introduced them to Valentino and Israel Martaan. The ShyWun's private guard.

35

Finally the big man himself walked in. His entrance was a shock, as he wore a black silk mask over his face. He greeted the blancos with a stoic nod.

Alvira found himself focusing on the only man in the room he could not see. He could tell from the shape of the mask that the man had a huge head. Below the black silk he wore Type A trappings of feudal dominance: a conservative dark vested suit with a beige silk shirt and dark tie, soft brown wing-tipped shoes. The hands were covered by white gloves. As he leaned forward, a platinum and diamond stickpin could be observed glistening upon his tie just above the huge belly line. Opulence effervesced in that overstated way one expects from royalty; a man born to a throne in some nether region, but that does not detract from his absolute rule. Alvira had the feeling he was observing a highly evolved voluptuary. A score of buttered virgins must accompany this quiet masked man to bed each night.

The man spoke softly, in clear English. "Chu tells us you are thinking of selling heroin in Alphabet City." Amazing how the voice came through the mask with such distinction. "If this is so, it is good that you come to us. Others have moved in without consulting us. But you have the wisdom, the respect. For that alone, you can consider yourselves among friends."

"A friend would show his face," Tommy blurted impulsively.

"A friend would not ask to see. I have made fortunes for men who have never seen my face."

"Sorry," T said. "I'm not used to—"

"No harm is taken. You are playing a game with no rules but ours, mine. If you don't wish to play, feel free to leave. You don't need us . . . do you?"

T shrugged. "We're staying. Go on, please."

"Who will supply your material?"

"We have sources set up," T said.

"Why not sell directly to us? We pay top dollar for pure."

"We want to get retail for it. We'll play it as you call it.

36

We're prepared to give you a fair price to operate. All you have to do is—"

"All we have to do is see that you are not killed or arrested instantly."

"Correct."

The masked man turned to Alvira. "The Alvira Kid. Your reputation on the street is straight up. You are a junkie, but unlike most, you would not betray a friend for a fix. You would rather be sick. Is that so?"

"Yes," Alvira said. How could he know about the incident last year, when the police tried to force Alvira to drop a dime on a connection by holding him sick in a cell?

"And you, Tommy Sparks. You could have worked with the heat and walked away from that kilo bust. Instead you did your time. These are not virtues we take lightly. Many come to us, every day, every month. Usually we say no, and they do it anyway. They are killed by their own crewmen or quickly ruined by the police. In your case—only because I feel you might succeed—we are prepared to help. If you agree to our terms, you will be given two points of activity. A storefront and an abandoned building. You will be permitted to run your crews without complications, unless you yourself draw heat or create conflict. Our fee for this will be one thousand dollars a day for the first week, two for the second, up to ten. If you are still alive and operating in ten weeks, we will stabilize the number for a while."

T shrugged. He didn't want to bicker. The offer was workable, and it was time to show class. No telling when he'd see this man again. Maybe only if something went wrong.

"Sounds good to me," he said, looking from ShyWun to Alvira.

Alvira shrugged. "Your play, T." T's cash and credit were providing seed action, so he had final say.

"Chu will be your crew boss," ShyWun said. "You can contact me through him."

"Very good."

"Your limit on material is ten percent heroin. Anything over and the deal is off. Have you been doing your market research?"

"Yes," Tommy said. "Your people are putting out the best bag around right now. Real dope. Seven to ten percent. Most of the others are putting out three percent laced with powdered barbiturate, injectable methadone, powdered Valium."

"Correct. We give people what they pay for. I trust you will do the same."

"Of course."

"You have my best wishes," ShyWun said, getting to his feet. "And now, if you will excuse me . . . "

They were ushered back into the van, deposited at the Jaguar. On the way home they blew reefers and listened to the Persuasions on the tape deck.

Alvira had an uncomfortable feeling. Something told him to back out now, before it was too late. But that was impossible. How would he get by? He was flat broke. Jones was upon him. For better or worse, he was in. He sniffled. Soon as they got back he'd hit T's stash and straighten out the bends and chills Jones was laying on him.

"What do you think, Alvira?" T asked.

"I think we're going to be in a whole lot of trouble soon or we're going to be rich." Alvira drew on a freebased reefer and closed his eyes.

Chu laughed in the back seat. "Don' worry," he said. "Eb'ry'sing bery bery cooool."

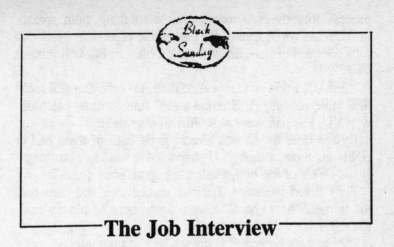

The Job Interview

JJ had no firsthand experience with smoking opium, so he and Furman turned to the resources of their drug library. They found the healing ritual described in a book called *Flowers in the Blood* and proceeded to invoke what Alexander Trocchi would call "the chemistry of alienation." *Flowers* was a sort of history book by a guy named Jeff Goldberg. Bless ol' Jeff, wherever and whoever, for layin' it out. The little glass alcohol burner would serve as a peanut-oil lamp. And hell, the coal bin was as good as any tent. They cooked the three grams of Chinaman JJ made in a deal, using a pristine shoe-polish can and the burner. With a long knitting needle JJ stirred the softening tar, watching it lighten slightly in color. He lifted a glob of it on the needle and placed it in the bowl of their converted hashish pipe. JJ held the pipe upside down so that the flame from the burner almost touched the opium pill. It crackled and bubbled, spreading out and sending up the sweet smoke.

"Das' ri', JJ! Git it up!"

JJ sucked until his eyes almost crossed. He repeated the

process four times before he felt a soothing calm spread through his wired frame. He passed the pipe.

"I donno, Furman, dis shit pack a hit . . . but will it hold ya'?"

"Shit, JJ, I don' wanna eat it, man, no way. Dat shit look like mule mucus, B. Smokin's mo' fun. Lemme catch up w'y'all." Furman went at it with all his might.

By the time the O was almost gone both of them had a righteous buzz, although JJ suspected it wouldn't last long. Just a tinkle of the bell. Pushin' no gone gong aroun'.

They heard footsteps. Furman leaned over and blew out the burner. "Mus' be ol' Frank. Shit, there be plenny coal out there."

"Shhh. Le's be sure." JJ drew a tiny .22 automatic.

"JJ, j'down there?"

"Who'z'at?"

"Shit, I don' know. Hol' on quiet."

"JJ! It's Chu! Hey, B!"

"Chu!" JJ stood up, allowing Chu to see his shadowed form. "I be ova heah, m'man!" He tucked the iron away.

"Wha'z shakin', nigga? M'main B!"

Chu chicken-bopped into the coal bin and greeted his young friend.

"Chu! Y'all'z lookin' gooood! Yo' a lean marine, jelly bean."

Chu's respect for JJ was due to an incident on the street years ago. Chu'd been tight with JJ's older bro', and the two of them were running a dime bag op in the South Bronx. JJ was a natural leader and was soon the youngest crew boss in unrecorded history. The Pennington brothers bought their momma a new Lincoln and rented her a huge spread in the black 'burbs so she could stow it. The number lasted five months before the lid blew. When the smoke cleared Chu saw it like this: JJ, walking with a number-twenty brown paper bag full of bundle packages, was spotted by some heat on stakeout. They told him to freeze. Instead he bolted into an abandoned building, ditched the

40

material, and surrendered indignantly. He was released. The bust was part of a sweep. Their headquarters and main stash were hit. Everyone was popped holding evidence, and they were almost cleaned out. But little JJ had his own cash stash as well as the bags he hid. That night he showed at the precinct with a lawyer and bondsman, bailed out his brother and Chu, and saved the day. So momma had to move back to the old pad, and bye-bye Lincoln. Still, JJ had proved his mettle.

"W'z happnin' w'chu, Chu?"

"I'm cool, JJ. Here to discuss a touch o' bizz. Who'z'at behin' j'?"

"'At's m'man. C'm ova heah, Furman, so Chu c'n check yo' face. Don' worry 'bou' m'baaad frien'. Me'n Furman eats off dee same plate!"

Furman stood up with a sheepish grin. "Hey, m'man, I heah all 'bout y'all fum JJ. Wanna suck on some o' dis Chinaman wi' me'n JJ? Got enough leff—"

"I got some'sin' fix you quicker than thee black smoke, B. Check it!" Chu dropped a bundle of Triad bags on the milk-crate-cum-table. Glassine flickered in candle light.

"Yowwweee! Santa Claus be comin' on a pound'a snow!"

"M'man Chu! Wha'z'at ch'all bringin' us heah?"

Chu pulled out a tiny tray, opened two bags dramatically with his spring knife, spilled the powder on the tray. He peeled a crisp one-hundred-dollar bill from a thick roll. He made lines with the blade, snorted two, passed the tray to JJ.

"J'dudes hab clean arms?"

"Sho'nuff!" JJ sniffed two lines and passed it on. "Tase gooood, Chu. Wha'z Triad mean?" He pointed to the logo stamped on the glassine bags.

"Tha'z m'new number, JJ. Like it?"

Furman hoofed his lines, rolled his eyes, and excused himself. He went to the far back corner, and they heard him puke.

"Wow! Dat nigga be gushin' like a mu'fuckin' volcano,

Jim, an' he ain' no pussycat! Dis mus' be some mean goodness you got heah, Chu." JJ cupped his balls and spread out for comfort. "Even *I* be catchin' a buzz."

Chu smiled. "JJ, j'high, B."

JJ smiled equally bright. "Yeah, but I'z gonna hol' onto mines." JJ turned to the corner where Furman was heaving. "Furman! Frank aks us not t'be makin' no mess heah. Shit, nigga, you is makin' dis place yo' vomitorium."

Furman moaned and gushed out another load. "Damn, dis be baaad shit, JJ. I be kissin' m'knees on dat one line."

JJ scratched his cheek with the back of his nails. "Yeah, dis mus' be yo' temple stash, daddy. 'Course, we w'z awready buzzin' on th' Chinaman, Chu. But nowhere neah dis high haid we gots now. What ch'do, Chu? Cut this heah dope w'mo' dope?"

Chu smiled. "Mmhmm. J'guys wanna work f'Triad?"

JJ suddenly caught the picture. It all made sense now. "Shit, Chu, you puttin' a crew togetha?"

"Mmhmm. Too bad j'bro'z in thee joint. But I fig' thee Pennington bro'z're righteous wi' me. Eef I can' work wi' Eddie I go f' his little B. J'c'n pull Furman in wi' j'eef j'trust'm straight up."

"Oh, hey, Chu. Furman be a baaad nigga. On'y thing Furman be sayin' t'fuzz is yesssa o' nooossa. An' Furman don' know what feah is, Jim. Even if he be sick he be cool. So wha'z the numba?"

"Rivington Street an' Alphabet City. Guys'll hab t'commute, but I c'n send a car an' hab j'driben back to Brooklyn afta sellin' the day's material."

"An' wha'z th' turn?"

"Turn hunred bundles a day. Gib j'a hunred salary an' commish'f j'cook'm out. Get busted an' I get Perrry Mason an' hab thee arresting officer demoted," Chu cackled. "An' Triad a smokin' bag, daddy. Sell out early ebery day. Cooo'?"

"Cooooo'."

"How'z 'bout Furman?"

"Furman wi' me, Chu. We be partners."

Chu winked and opened another bag. "Well, then j'is no longer unemployed niggas. J'pockets gonna jingle."

JJ looked reflective. "But Chu, is you protected on dem streets? Mean scene. Bein blood don' mean squat in dat savage monkey scene."

Chu shrugged. "We wi' thee ri' people, bu' no guarantees. Cova j'back." He looked from JJ to Furman. "Cova each otha good. Frien's make j'safe."

"How long Triad be workin'?"

"Not long. We yus' warmin' up. Got mucho material. Caliente! I'm runnin' thee whole crew, B, an' j'know I run a lean machine."

"Furman, you listnin'? M'bean run a lean machine! You on?"

"Sho'nuff!"

"Like the sound?"

"I'z w'chu, m'main brain, JJ."

JJ shook Chu's hand. "When we start?"

"I'll send the car tomorrow, 'bou' seben-thirty a.m. That cool wi' Furman?"

"Coooo', B. I be meetin' you," Furman said, still hunched over with the heaves. For a sick man he sure looked happy.

"How'z 'bout 'f m'driver pick j'up ri' outside thees building?"

"Cooo'."

"Cooo'."

"Cooo'. So le's knock off uno mo' bag an' I gots t'split."

"I ain' goin' neah dat shit," Furman groaned.

Chu and JJ cackled.

"An' JJ, j'work wi' me befo'n hip Furman to thee sco'. No tracks on thee arms, man, an' no nods on thee job. Do la cura an' keep it chilled out. This'z serious bizz."

"M'hip, m'man."

43

Chu started for the door after hooting another line.

"Hey, Chu! You leff yo' bags an' yo' bill behin'," JJ said. He lifted a rolled-up hundred caked with powder.

"Tha's f'm'new crewmen, JJ. See j'moonyana. Thee car will be an ol' red Eldo, an' m'man Ya Ya be drivin'. 'Member Ya Ya?"

"Spanish light-skin bleed use t'work yo' scene in th' Bronx, ri'?"

"Mmhmm. Good frien' o' j'bro. He be glad j'comin' in wi' us."

"Cooo'." JJ made a thumbs-up and smiled as Chu split.

"Hey, Furman, c'mon outa dat cawna, you messy nigga. You jus' puked yo' way through yo' firs' job interview."

> **In the Great Serenade of things,**
>
> **Am I the most cancelled passage?**
>
> —Gregory Corso

Eric Shomberg had been driving around in circles through the rain-splashed seedy streets of Alphabet City. Rows of war-torn buildings, broken dirty concrete, open smoking sewers. Oil drum fires were speckled around, bearing signatures of the lotus crews. He made a face from LaTuna. Maybe. Things changed quickly on the street. It was worth a quick sound. He parked the cab on Avenue B and walked a few blocks to Third and C. It was a red-brick tenement teeming with shadows and junkie life. Eric watched from the corner for a few minutes. Every so often a cluster of junkies would waft out and split up, peering around nervously. Other customers walked around the block over and over, hearing, "Red light! Keep walkin'," from the lookout until he told them to enter. Clearly he was instructed to avoid a large buildup in front of the tenement. It wasn't working. At least fifteen blancos were hovering around outside, rubbing their noses, walking in place, jabbering, scratching, sniffling.

Eric couldn't invest the time—at least a half-hour by his take—necessary to cop. But he couldn't not cop either.

45

He'd only put fifty bucks on the meter, and it was almost three in the afternoon. He had to hustle or the dispatcher would be giving him the standard reprimand, maybe even cutting his workdays. All he needed was a nice cooker full of the Rx and he would be able to sit calmly on that seat and watch the cake roll in as the city rolled by like a loony tune. Without it he was fucked. He'd have to go home early and wrap himself up in blankets to offset the chills that were gaining on him. He'd not be able to venture far from the porcelain lest his stomach drop out. And how could he be expected to negotiate midtown traffic with his nerves exposed? He'd had a wake-up ready for the morning but banged it last night to come off some speedy C a fellow cabbie sold him.

Fuckin' taxi shit. Gotta have eyes all over. Bozos cuttin' in front of you. Buses don't give a flyin' shit. You have to watch the turkey sittin' behind you. He'd been taken at gunpoint twice since the beginning of his involuntary career as a Manhattan hack. Arbitrary picking up was sheer kamikaze shit, and he didn't intend to place himself in that situation again. He wasn't prejudiced against blacks or PRs. Not even slightly. Any preconditioning he might've had that instinctified bigotry was quickly negated in the 'Nam jungles, where he learned that if blood from a black man's arm could save you, you took the donation and thanked him. But rolling a taxi through Harlem or East New York made him ten times more nervous than combat in the tropics. Fact is, in 'Nam he learned for the first time how to really relax. Thanks to Mr. Jones, son of Somnus, the Father of Sleep. No kinder, more understanding gentleman walked the face of the earth. There'd been an opium den not more than a few blocks from base in Saigon. Regal and illegal. A dreamlike interior insulated the little sleepy hollow from outside realities. Pappa-san was only too happy to take his money, escort him to a cot, and summon the chef. The chef was a thin Vietnamese sleepwalker of about forty with the smooth face of a sedated baby, wearing a tattered

U.S. Army shirt that said "Goldstein" on the name tag, red P.F. Flyers sneakers, and loose-fitting cotton trousers. He would appear with a brass tray and begin the ritual.

Due to metabolics and temperament, Eric quickly went from six to twenty pipes at a sitting. This was necessary to achieve the relief and exquisite suspension of ego he'd come to expect. He could not resist the sweet ambiguity of opium, the way it softened the real world without negating it altogether like booze did. It was an aesthetic, getting high, and it pleased him beyond petty feelings of accomplishment and all that other tribal corn. Eric had no fixed idea of what constituted contentment, but he sensed the factors to be internal, subjective, decentralized. Before he was shipped back to the States, Eric was up to fifty pipes at a nightly lay. He and the Chinaman were partners in paradise. Bunk mates.

He hit the street and found out quickly that those little bags barely touched him. Weak excuse for dope in the States. In order to maximize profits the bosses cut it to shit and back. It took a bundle just to give him a buzz. He found a doctor who wrote him a standard script for Percodans, so he went on to think of other things. He worked as a carpenter. When properly medicated Eric could be fastidious. He'd started college before 'Nam, so returned on the GI bill. Majored in psychology and did well. Then the DEA fixed it so a doctor couldn't write for Percs anymore without going through mucho red tape and pressure to keep it down. Illegal to treat addicts. A police, not a medical problem. Ol' Doc threw him over. Back to the street. High prices and poor quality. He took a gig—the taxi—but barely got by. Then the Shah of Iran was deposed by the Ayatollah Khomeini, and the streets of New York filled up with some very fine and cheap Persian heroin. The competition from the Golden Triangle had to raise quality and lower prices to maintain market. For the first time in a dozen years street dope was on the money, and scoring was wide open. Eldridge Street off Houston was lined with working PR social clubs, just like the black clubs uptown. Eric could fix for twenty bucks, and another ten got him high. At first. Now it took him five bags. Half a bundle. Fifty bucks. The shit was good, and it was easy to get a nasty Jones with prices so reasonable. With his gig and a little dealing he could do it, usually. When things got bad his Jones kicked him right in the nervous system. But when things were right Eric Shomberg felt good about life. He didn't have time for college anymore but stayed informed with reading lists.

"Red light! Come back in twenny minutes," the lookout hissed.

"I can't come back, man, I'm workin'. But I'll slip you a dime for express."

The lookout smiled. They can smell it. He held out his hand, and Eric laid a ten on the palm. "Go buy it. Walk the stairs up to the third floor."

As soon as Eric entered the building he could sense that something wasn't right. When LaTuna worked a building they allowed only their own people to loiter in the lobby. These dark conduits were stuffed with vagrants. How come they weren't kicked out? Okay, so it wasn't LaTuna. That didn't mean there wasn't good dope to be scored. Maybe this was a new op putting their best foot forward. He resisted an impulse to bolt and walked past the lobby crowd. Going up the stairs, he met a few impalpable forms coming down.

"How's it running?"

"What d'y'expect?"

Eric shrugged. Not exactly encouraging, but if people were buying it must be decent. He continued up. On the third floor there was a line and a bagman, but no one working the line, no one keeping things orderly. A fly-by-night op if ever. He caught a glimpse of one of the bags as a guy stuffed a bundle in his pocket. They had dark brown tape sealing them. LaTuna bags were always sealed with clear tape. Eric got on line and waited, hoping for the best.

A few moments later he copped his half-bundle and headed out. It was on the second landing that he realized it hadn't been wise to cop this way, good dope or not. He saw a scuffle in an abandoned apartment, probably a customer being taken off. Eric sped up. LaTuna buildings were protected. That is, the crews would see to your safety while you were in their area. Muggings were bad for bizz, and the rodents knew that taking off a LaTuna customer, even a blanco, could get your ass handed to you. This crew had no such provisions. He was on his own.

On the ground floor he passed a few desperados seemingly on their way up. They surrounded him and sprang blades suddenly. He felt cold steel up against his neck. Without turning, he knew what would be there.

"Come wi' me o' j'get cut," the man said.

There were three of them, one looking nastier than the next. They were sick, crazed, not to be played with. They led him under the stairwell, took his half-bundle, money, subway tokens, cigarettes, ring. One of them spilled the contents of his wallet on the floor, another took off his watch. The third admired his sneakers for a second before suggesting he take them off.

"Just leave me one bag, please. I'm sick," he pleaded.

The man with the knife looked at his tracks, frowned, dropped one bag into Eric's sweaty palm. "Here, dope fien'."

There were two sealed gimmicks in his denim jacket, and mercifully they only took one.

"Stay here, m'fucka, o' we keel jou!"

They walked out of the building. Eric looked around in the near darkness. The man who'd stolen his sneakers had left behind a very badly worn pair of archaic sixties "Beatles boots." Eric put them on. Despite what was happening he felt impending relief. . . .

He clutched the bag in his sweating fist. He had to do it now! Eric dropped water from his kit into the bent spoon. He opened the bag and watched the powder break up in the

49

cooker. God pointed the weeper's sharp tip into the main-line on the first attempt.

Sweeeet jizz of Jesus! Jumpin' Jesuits! That fly-by-night was a smoker! No wonder the muggers were workin' it. The relief came immediately, and he felt a wave of optimism inappropriate to his condition. He tapped his pocket for a cigarette and looked at his watch, remembered both were gone. Didn't seem to matter terribly. The boots stopped pinching his feet . . . it seemed.

He waited awhile and walked out of the building. He saw the three jerks who took him leaning on a car. Probably just split up his cash and bags. One smiled at him, and Jones made him smile back before catching himself. Big joke. It was their street, and they feared no one. Surely not some pale-eyed blanco punk dope fiend.

Eric limped back to the taxi and got in. With a little luck he could work up the price of a few more bags of that great shit. For the moment he was cool. He could swing with it! No stopping him. He could drive barefoot!

> The mind is its own place, and in itself
>
> Can make a heav'n of hell, a hell of heav'n. . . .
>
> —Lucifer in Milton's *Paradise Lost*

Dave Skully emerged from the subway on Delancey Street and blinked in the light of day. He walked over to Rivington Street and the Bowery, where he'd copped a bundle of splendid Triad goodness the other day. Hope they're still on. Best bee-zag on the street.

The door to the building was open, but no one around. Inside, the big steel door—new and incongruous with the dilapidated texture of the old building—was locked. He rapped, but there was no answer. Shit! When a brand really swings they sell out early. Triad was becoming a famous smoker.

Skully was a few hours away from severe withdrawal but determined not to panic. He didn't have to show at his bartending gig in the Bronx for another few hours. Plenty of cake in his pockets, and after all this *was* New York City and it shouldn't be too hard to locate another score. Skully bopped over to Chinatown and into a teahouse near Chatham Square looking out on the old Five Points. He contemplated the next move over hot tea and a taste of dim sum. Shit! Have to track through Alphabet City.

Walking out onto the sunny pavement, he flicked his butt into the gutter. Started tasting harsh. That meant his system was in dire need of the Sacred Substance. In a matter of an hour he'd be sweating, shivering, nervous, raw, and his bowels would begin to explode. In the restaurant he'd split his cake so that one hundred was in his pocket and another in his sock. He carried no wallet or keys. He put his spring knife in the waistband of his jeans where the denim jacket would cover it and began the hike.

Seemed to be more la hara than vendadors. Shit. A bad day. Dave rapped to a few faces who looked familiar. No one knew where the Triad people might be until he asked a young tattooed dude he'd first mistaken for someone else. The cat looked familiar and said he knew where to score.

"Gotta take a walk."

A light sun shower fell as they turned the corner of Eighth and C. They were walking towards Avenue D.

"This is Green Tape around here," Dave said, getting suspicious. Tattoo had asked for a bag commission, and Dave had agreed. But he didn't want to pay if the guy was taking him to Green Tape. Everyone knew where they were and could score without any expensive outside help.

"Triad here too," the man said.

That was strange. Not run by the same people, and it would take three bags of Green to put you where one Triad put you. Unlikely the Green Tape crew would tolerate that sort of competition under their noses.

Skully got the distinct feeling he didn't like what was goin' down. He began scanning nervously for a graceful exit. "Shit, man, I think I'm gonna sound on that dude over there," he told Tattoo. "I know that cat and maybe—"

"Come wi' me," the man insisted, his voice soft but menacing.

Skully hedged. If he started to walk the man might jump him, even knife him, and no one would interfere. He was white, and they'd just step over his corpse and do bizz as usual until the ambulance arrived.

Skully became aware of another dude who'd been following them. The first dude rapped to a few loitering PRs in Spanish.

Skully could see the equation, the dudes looking him over. Time to book.

"Yo, poppa! Where in fuckin' hell j'goin'?"

Two arms came around his back, holding him tight. He was spun around. Tattoo pointed to the shell of a building.

"In there, man. Moob' it!"

No weapons visible, but Skully stood in the center of too many mean-looking honchos to mess around.

"No need to get tough," he said, amazed at his own resignation. He pulled the wad out of his pocket. "Here's m'money. Just leave me alone."

Tattoo snapped Skully's roll but still insisted he enter the building.

"Jacket off," one of them said, showing a cheap pistol.

"Hey, you got m'fuckin' money!"

"Shut up. Git it off!"

The sleazoid picked up Skully's jacket, took a pack of butts out of the breast pocket, divided them with his associates.

"Now pants, man."

"What?"

The shiv fell to the floor, and soon the rest of Skully's cake was in their hands.

"Rapido! Green gonna sell out. Le's split!"

One stayed behind long enough to tie Skully's jeans into knots. When he was satisfied that his victim would need ten minutes to untie the legs, he dropped the jeans on the garbage-carpeted floor and stalked out.

Yen chills ran up and down Skully's spine, distracting him. He tried to undo one of the tighter knots, but his hands shook uncontrollably. A coughing fit gripped him, and he held his chest. Weak, he sat on garbage and broken glass, shielded only by his skivvies. He could hear a Crazy Eddie commercial roaring out of a ghetto blaster somewhere close by, and the harshness irritated him unbearably. One of the jerks had left a burning cigarette—his—on the floor. He lifted it to his quivering lips.

They'd cleaned him. How the fuck could he smile and mix drinks in this condition? He thought about a book he'd read in the joint, by Kafka, called *The Metamorphosis*. Gregor Samsa wakes up one morning and discovers he's a cockroach. The superlative problem is: *How can I put my human clothes on this body so I can go to work?*

He didn't even have a dime to call the bar and offer an excuse. Didn't have the price of a subway token. Now, ain't Fate a fucking? Too bad Gregor couldn't join him at the moment. It took awhile, but he got the knots out, put on his jeans, and hit the street.

"How many j'want? Las' call on Green Tape."

He turned and faced a green-capped crew worker.

"None," he said. "I just got taken off."

The worker shrugged. "Betta git some money, poppa. J'lookin' seeek."

"Yeah! Got a smoke?"

The worker told him to stop shaking as he lit the cigarette. "Cop some dinero an' come back aks f' Baba. I make sure j'don' git taken again."

Skully took the spring knife out of his pocket and showed it to Baba. "Hey, B, I know it's a bit tarnished, but the spring is good. Clean an' sharpen it. Wanna give me two bags for it?"

"That no open from thee front, poppa. I no like—"

"One bag! Man, I'm sick as shit. That's all I have. I gotta go to work!"

"So come back lata."

"Can't. I work in the Bronx. If I don't show I'm fucked. Gimme one bag and a token for the train and it's yours."

Baba clicked the blade out and examined it. It was dull and dirty but would take an edge.

"Wai' here. I get j'uno bag Green Tape. J'gotta gimmick?"

54

"Yeah," Skully said, feeling the anticipation of relief.

"Green run good today. J'be fine," Baba said. He ducked out and slid down the basement where the Green Tape crew stored their material. He came back and led Skully into the building he'd been mugged in. "There's a gallery upstairs, poppa, bu' dey charge three bucks. We go in here. Nobody in this dump."

They walked up one flight and into a rank empty apartment. Skully could hear activity above them. Baba turned on a water faucet, and Skully started to prepare. The cylinder of his gimmick was cracked. He borrowed Baba's dirty weeper and started to probe for a line. He was shaking too badly, and Baba had to hit him. Baba's long thin fingers moved deftly, fluidly. He had a practiced doctor's touch.

The eyelids came down lightly before the point was out of Skully's arm. He felt his muscles losing tension and pain. His breathing cleared. Baba lit a fresh butt and put it to Skully's lips. The blanco poked hungrily.

"That Green is gooood today," said lazy lips.

"Da' shit's good 'cause Triad come out wi' a smoker! Gotta keep up."

Skully was starting to feel like himself again.

"Hey, Baba, m'name's Skully."

Baba nodded. Calm eyes said, "So what?"

"You helped me, hombre. I wanna pay you back. I know that blade's no bargain. Listen, if you take the subway up to the Bronx tonight and bring me a bundle, I'll tip you two bags and you'll drink for free. I'm a bartender."

Baba brightened. "Soun' good, man. Where j'bar?"

"Take the train to Two Twenty-fifth. Walk over to the Concourse. Ask anybody for Mimm's Cafe. I go on in a few hours, so make it."

"Cool," Baba said, handing Skully change for a subway token.

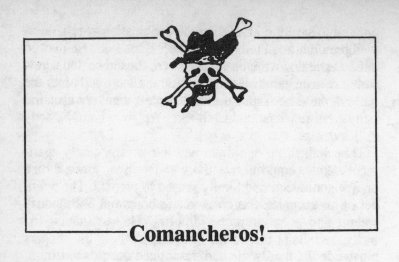

Comancheros!

The Rivington Street spot drew heat due to gunplay on Chu's part, squashing a holdup attempt. It stayed closed three weeks. The partners were pushing to reopen. The ShyWun thought it premature, but when T sounded the fact that they were turning seventy to eighty grand a day there, the masked man softened. And raised his tax.

Four days after the grand opening a wide four-door pitted Plymouth—looked like a fallen gypsy cab—pulled up outside. Chu saw it from inside and wondered about the four men sitting in it. Latins, mid-thirties, too hefty to be junkies and too sloppy to be heat. He turned to his assistant.

"Get thee las' customers out an' lock thee door, Pepe!"

Pepe'd just barely touched the tumbler on the big steel door when it was thrown open from outside. The force knocked Pepe to the ground. He turned over, blade flashing, screaming, "Chu! Chu!"

One of the intruders leveled a silenced pistol in his extended arms, lifting it to eye level as Pepe flung his blade. The handle hit the man's shoulder, just offsetting his aim

56

enough to save the Triad's life. A bullet spit into the wood wall beside him.

Chu appeared with his silenced .32, ducked behind a garbage can, and assumed firing position. He opened up in the narrow hallway. The closest intruder caught lead in the belly as Pepe ran behind Chu.

"Chu, man, day gonna keel us. C'mon. I know a ways outa heah."

"We gonna hold'm."

"We gonna die!"

One of the men set off a gas canister, ending the conversation. They were equipped with masks and charging.

"Git us outa heah!"

Pepe led Chu up to the third floor, pointing out the fishing wire strung across assorted stairs to trip up anyone in pursuit who didn't know the layout. Silent bullets whizzed around as they leaped out a window, down a ledge to the second floor, dropping from there down into a lot full of broken glass and debris. They left behind over six grand in cake, twenty bundles of Triad material, and a Comanchero corpse.

The stiff's wallet told tales, but in fragments. Its owner was Comanchero, at any rate. References to a Rafael permeated the scribbled notes and lists. Questions float out onto the street.

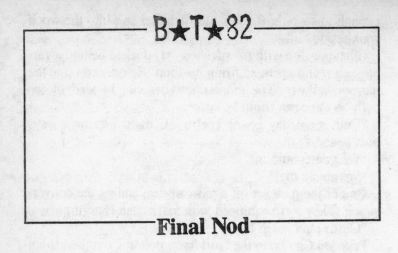

Final Nod

JJ watched the prowlers turn the corner of Stanton Street off the Bowery. As soon as they were out of sight he walked over to Rivington. Triad'd been opening on and off on Riv due to excessive heat. But Furman was covering the Avenue D spot, and JJ only had a few bundles to sell. Things looked open on Rivington, so he set up and began to tout.

A familiar blanco wearing dark shades bopped over and bought a bag, then returned ten minutes later and took a bundle. "Shit's still on the money," he said. "Amazing."

JJ said, "Triad always the same smokin' bag," without looking at the blanco. He was preoccupied with selling out and makin' it back to Brooklyn to enjoy his evening cura.

The prowler returned, moving slowly down Rivington and stopping outside the storefront Dr. Nova sometimes worked. JJ was across the street in the doorway of a punk club. He made Chico the Cop in the front seat of the car. Chico was born on these streets and had the rep of a man who did not play. Looked like they were sticking around, so JJ ascended a long creaky flight of stairs, paid three bucks, entered the punk club.

There was a band playing loud, unmelodious music. Blanco girls with tight jeans, makeup, and spiked hair nodded metronomically to the beat. The guys were mostly greased and leathered. An occasional Mohawk. JJ was one of the few dark faces in the loft, but no one looked twice.

He stationed himself by the window so he could watch the man across the street. Their presence would scare away customers. Shit.

"Looks like they're gonna hang out."

He turned to face the voice. It belonged to a blanco, maybe twenty, wearing a black satin shirt, white duck pants, black engineer boots, and a Roseland d.a. "Fuckin' cops. How's a man supposed to turn a buck?"

JJ shrugged. "I donno."

The guy got closer. JJ could smell his sweat and chewing gum. "Listen, I know the score. I buy bags on the street all the time."

"Zat so?"

"Yeah. I've seen you aroun' too." The punk's eyes glistened with inebriation, from the smell JJ guessed alcohol.

"Naww. I ain't fum rou' heah."

"You know where I can score some D, don't you?"

"I donno nothin' like that."

"Hey, I'm not heat. Loosen up, baby, nobody gonna bother you here. Tell you what, I'll give you thirty bucks for two."

JJ shrugged, looked around, checked the punk's face. What the hell. "Meet me in that corner over there," he said, turning and walking off.

The punk assumed position. JJ took the thirty and dropped two bags into his hand.

"These ain't dummies, are they?"

"No way. They sealed an' stamped Triad, man. Where you been?" Almost everyone knew those bags.

"Do me a favor. Wait 'til I get off. If I like it I'll buy all you have on you."

"Can't stick aroun' too long, Jim."

59

"Gimme five. Just got to borrow a spike and get off in the bathroom."

"Hurry."

JJ went back to his vigil by the window. Damn, that band was bad. Not good-baaad but *evil*. Rank! Desecration of Soul!

The band stopped finally, and the room lost its jump. JJ was grateful, toking on a butt and watching the cops just hanging out like they had nothing to do. No wonder so much crime goes down in this city.

A sudden shriek caused JJ to turn around. There was a spike-haired girl in the middle of the floor, howling her brains out. Some guys were trying to cool her, but she just kept it up. What the fuck was she howling about? Something about "Dead!" "He's *dead*!" Shit. Probably somebody checked out from listening to that evil rock band. Well, at least they're not playing.

A crowd was forming near the bathroom. JJ wondered if . . . nawwww. Couldn't be. He walked over to see what was happening.

There, on the dance floor, was his new customer. The punk was stone blue, mouth and neck covered with vomit. A dude was pounding his heart but after awhile gave up. "Dead," he said softly.

"Call the cops!" someone let out.

"The cops are on the street outside," another dude said. "I'll go get'm!"

"No, I'll go!" JJ huffed. He bolted out the door and didn't stop running 'til he was back in Alphabet City.

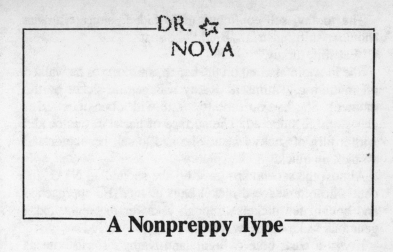

DR. ☆
NOVA

A Nonpreppy Type

Kathy McQueen had to sell a few more bags of reefer before calling it a day. She was down for five but needed six bags of Triad to soothe the monkey. If Triad was sold out she'd have to go for a lesser bag, maybe not even get really straight. Nothing came near Triad. Straight-up goodness! If bad news fell she'd need a full bundle of anything else.

Her clear blue eyes were alive, darting across Washington Square Park. One for the police and the other for customers. Pressure was on. It was getting late, and she had the shorts. Mercy!

A dark man looked at her flirtatiously, commenting on her blonde hair. He pursed his lips and made pussy-sucking noises. Kathy snarled and gave him the thumbs-down sign.

He was persistent.

"What ch'doin', momma? Y'all sellin' them long pretty legs?"

"Beat it, pig-ugly turd!"

"What'z'a matta, baby, got somethin' agin' black men?"

"No, just ugly men."

The toothy, self-confident smile faded, along with the shoulder-shifting strut. "Bitch!" he spat.

"Eat shit, turkey."

She lit a joint and sat on the bench, smirking as he walked off muttering to himself. Kathy was getting sicker by the moment. She had no time to waste with obnoxious jerks. Her stomach fluttered. The surface of her skin was coated with a film of sticky sweat. She had to sell her reefer and go pick up quick.

Almost the second she gave up she spotted an NYU student who often scored nickel bags off her. He approached and bought ten nickels. Enough cake for the night and a generous wake-up! Now tell me there ain't a God.

It was a clear blue twilight, and Kathy's spirits rose as she walked east towards Sixth and C. It was still early enough, if she was lucky. Her bones ached, and she considered a taxi, but that would cut severely into her scoring funds.

On Sixth and B she caught her reflection in a store window. Tight blue sweater over her trim, small-breasted form, faded blue jeans hugging around the hips and long legs. She examined her short dirty-blonde hair. A year on heroin had done nothing negative to her looks. She'd lost weight and looked tight and lean. It was inside that the price had been paid to Mr. Jones. Inside, where her whole being ached for Lotus Land.

A year ago Kathy had been a second-year art student at Cooper Union. She was fascinated by the punk scene and had a weakness for musicians. When she met Terry one night at CBGB, she couldn't get over his trashy cool.

Terry was a skinny fallen Catholic angel. He was naughty as sin and liked loud rock music and strong heroin. Kathy had a deep affinity for people who don't do what they're told. Terry was the very manifestation of this attitude. He moved in with her a few days after they met. A week of fucking their brains out didn't diminish the fire. Her crib turned into a teacup scene for his friends, many of them celebrities on the punk music scene. They got along fine with Kathy. Everyone thought she was cool and dug her paintings.

But two months into the scene Terry took a fall for possession. It took three days to raise bail. When she picked him up she hardly recognized him. The eyes were dead, dull, defeated. He'd been junk-sick to the max and was almost crippled with pain. He smelled of death.

They returned to the crib, and Kathy fixed him promptly. But Terry's tolerance had diminished, and he o.d.'d on his usual dose. Kathy had never seen an o.d. She didn't have the first idea how to help.

Terry was dead when the ambulance arrived, leaving behind his highly addicted girlfriend to fend for herself. But she was smart and street wise. She found a girl dealer who gave her bagged nickels of reefer up front and hipped her how to pass it and score dope with the proceeds. It was a real education. Much more demanding and rewarding than Cooper Union, where consequence was less immediate and dense with abstraction. Everything else became petty in the face of heroin. Simply nothing in the world like it. It liberated her from the tribal madnesses of competitiveness, inherent hostilities, even sex. She found her point of view shifting in what seemed like a practical, even pleasant way.

Weekly phone calls to her parents in Jersey had always been painful and frustrating. But on the goodness she could call and babble cheerfully. It mattered little that she couldn't relate to her market-analyst father and secretary mother. Empty-headed suburban mystics. That's what she thought of them. Their fancy props and hysterical inevitability made her ill. But on dope she could sound loving for ten minutes. Without the slightest effort she could dream up intricate explanations for how she was spending her time. No, she was not attending classes. Her faculty adviser fully approved of an independent study program, and of course she would receive credits after completing a series of paintings. And she was supplementing the income Daddy sent her by selling an occasional painting. That part of her tale was true. A few of Terry's musician friends were making money. She'd offered three paintings for a total of seven hundred bucks. That's seventy bags! No small score! She was still painting sometimes, when she had enough stashed to sit still.

The glowing phone calls to Jersey paid off. Daddy upped the ante from fifty to a hundred bucks per week. Kathy had her own room in a pad she shared with two other Cooper students, and her portion of the rent was small. She ate like a bird, particularly on heroin. A mere twenty bucks weekly took care of food.

Kathy had style enough to look hip without spending money. She rarely had to pay admission or buy her own drinks at the punk clubs. She was a long way from desperation. Except for dope. It put pressure on her. Made her count pennies. It forced her to deal reefer and risk not only arrest but her ass as well.

Kathy looked up. She wondered if the three young PRs bopping her way were going to surround her and take her off.

Her hand slid into her jacket pocket and closed around a can of Mace. But they were content to make sucking noises as she passed.

"OOOooOoO mometta!"

"Flacita! Petita!"

Kathy ignored them. The Triad spot on C was in a building and kept no touters on the street, so it was hard to tell if they were open. She walked up to the storefront and rapped on the door. An eyeball peered back at her through the peephole. The door swung open. Kathy was a regular, and her face was well known.

"Hey, Chu! Got a bundle for me?"

He smiled and dropped the package in her hand.

She paid him. "You have a gimmick, Chu? I'm really feelin' like shit tonight."

"Don' sell gimmicks. Go roun t'Third an' D."

"Thanks," she said, "but I don't like goin' near those guys."

"I know what j'mean. Pretty girl gots no business on that street. When m'frien' come back I send him t'get a weeper. Yus' si'down'n hang out."

"How nice of you." She flashed her man-melter smile at him.

Kathy was impatient to get straight and was about to open and sniff a bag when Chu handed her a tinfoil pipe and told her to draw on the tip when he lit it. The acrid smell of burning goodness filled her lungs at once. She'd never smoked before and was amazed at how quickly it went to her head.

After a few deep, satisfying hits, Chu lit a joint of strong Thai reefer sprinkled liberally with heroin. A far cry from the harsh commercial 'lumbo reefer she was used to. And the dope didn't hurt, either.

As they sat, a man came in, bought bags, and slipped out. Chu placed the cake in a box full of money.

"Wow!" Kathy said.

"Hmm. Mucho dinero. Not mines though, baby. Me yus' a workin' man."

"Doin' better than most, I'd say."

He took the compliment gracefully, with a broad smile.

Another man walked in. He slapped Chu's palm and said, "Wha'z happnin'?"

"Go roun' t'D an' pick up a weeper f'm'frien'" Chu said.

Kathy tried to hand the man a five, but Chu waved her down.

"On me, baby, f'brightnin' m'day."

"Be ri' back," the man said.

The heroin they'd smoked was hitting nicely, so she sat down feeling calm, watching Chu deal with the assortment of customers walking in and out. An old Dylan record— from the preholy days—was playing on the radio. "They stone you just like they said they would." Chu, as far as she could see, was emotionally immune to the fact that he was risking prison, a holdup, or any number of things that can and do go wrong in the dope business.

She admired his fluid style and animation. His act was very together. Crisp. He took cake and doled out bags with a true economy of energy. All the while his eyes and ears were tuned for trouble. Sometimes, when he leaned over to reach for something, she could see the print of a pistol through his thin brown leather jacket. He was a strong contrast to her preppy friends from another lifetime. Also from her trendy musician types. He was *right there*! On the money like a good bang of Triad.

Kathy hung out until Chu sold his last bag and closed up shop, by which time he was getting a strong intuition that she found him desirable. He swept her into his newly purchased five-year-old Eldo, left her in the double-parked car as he made his cash drop at the Tompkins Square crib.

Kathy slid a Bush Tetras cassette out of her handbag and into the slot on the dashboard. She sat back smoking a joint, feeling the butter-soft leather under her sharp ass. It was the first time since Terry she felt at ease with a man.

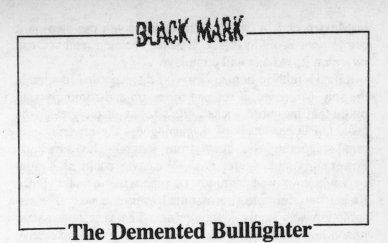

The Demented Bullfighter

Rafael was not born the mean son of a bitch he was. It was something he learned. Something he picked up in the early years of his criminal career. Born in Juárez but raised in Mexico City and later L.A., he found in his early teens that he was a capable businessman in a very unique position. He had blanco associates in and around L.A. who would pay highball cake for good opium and heroin. He had Mexican hombres in the trade on the supply end who thought nothing of giving him material on credit. He was bilingual, bi-coastal, and well connected on both sides.

Rafael opened up a quickly expanding op: strong brown Mexican junk cut with Nestlé's Quik. The money gushed in. Karl Marx woulda puked.

But the heroin business has always been a lesson in nastiness, and even with his close Mex hombres there were problems. If they scored a ki and were used to putting a six hit on it, they threw the six, even if it killed the quality. Pure can be hit maybe ten times. But commercial material has already been hit. The way the trade works is: How cheap can I get it, and how many times can I cut it? Score in Mexico or L.A. and you're lucky if you can step on it one to one. Score in Persia, Burma, Thailand, and you can *dance* on it. No one will complain.

Rafael's faith in human behavior disintegrated like ice in the sun. Moreover, it seemed to the up-and-coming young pirate that the more wicked one's behavior the greater the take. On upper levels of disgustingness the rewards were mind-staggering. He knew from watching his suppliers. Power, privilege, force, flash. Whatever could be bought . . . whatever was wittingly or otherwise for sale. Since Rafael was for sale, he assumed everyone was. The assumption was rarely inappropriate. The year he went to prison he read that President Nixon had granted executive clemency to a racketeer named Jimmy Hoffa. Later Nixon was granted clemency in turn by President Ford. Rafael felt himself to be in good company as a criminal. Crime makes the world go round. Perhaps one day he too would make history and be granted executive clemency.

Rafael had another gift besides subjective observation. He had *presence*. He could speak, smile, glare, frown, and strut with an air of absolute power, of graceful and naive self-confidence. He had life by the balls. Even if he was occasionally shot at. His hard face exuded command.

The L.A. blancos ate it up. Had they been familiar with Manhattan pimps, they might've snickered. Instead they mythologized him and his dope. He was Sportin' Life, and his stash was Happy Dust. His veneered presence fit right into the Hollywood Hills, Venice, Westwood scenes. These people did not distinguish between graceful and slick. They hardly distinguished between honest and lookin' good.

Rafael moved as much heroin and cocaine as he could get his highly financed and hyperconnected hands on. He took a small but well-placed estate in the Hollywood Hills, doing business from a living room looking out on miles of lights, landscape, and lesser players down there running around like ants: rows of blue-collar bedrooms fenced in by highways and arteries. Conduits of electricity pulsing away actively, in sharp contrast to Rafael's languid inertia as he sat back on the sofa to nod with his head full of heroin and his ears full of Chicano bebop. He mirrored the walls, commissioned a rosewood table with platinum inlay, and placed upon it a solid gold antique gunpowder scale. It was the shrine of his religious worship, turning brown powder into green dinero.

He made his own special bags. Nonporous papers, a painfully fancy fold, covered with plastic and shrink-sealed. Each package had a red sombrero logo and the word *Siesta* stamped on it. Fifties, hundreds, two-hundreds, four-hundreds. But he wasn't dealing in no school yard, poppa. The fours went fastest.

Then suddenly things got weird. It started with small details, but soon affected everything. A distant associate got busted. No one Rafael did steady bizz with, but his name was in the dude's address book. There was much talk of heat. Rafael's heroin chippy flared into a raging Jones from worry. One of his steady sources lost a shipment. They made up their losses by selling weaker dope. Rafael refused to buy it; he became an unreliable dealer because he often had no stock. When his suppliers re-upped strong shit they refused to front him because he hadn't helped them recoup. The strong material went to those who did, on credit. Rafael had to pay cash for weaker shit.

He lost customers. They cleaned up or found other scores. One by one the props went. Cars, motorcycles. The house was next. A few accounts owed him cash—people he'd partied with just a short while ago—but they weren't coming through. He'd never bothered to save a nickel. Lots of cake passed through, but most of it went up his arm or through his nose. Ayyy caramba!

Then he had a visitor, an Italian dude he dealt coke to. He knew the man only as "Dino." One of the few who paid on delivery. The guy was having a cash-flow problem. Dino owed an Italian coke factor one hundred grand. The man told him if he didn't pay up in one week he'd be dead. Since Rafael knew both men, maybe he could lay some reason on the matter.

Rafael had a better idea.

"Tell j'what, amigo. J'owe'm a hunred. I keel heem f'feefty."

The man smiled and told Rafael he'd have the cake for him in two days tops. Muchas gracias.

It was Rafael's first plunge into really quick money. Dealing was profitable, but you had to work, scheme, sweat, even socialize. Mayhem better suited his temperament.

A new, vicious regime kicked in. He drifted into a Pachuco crime family and quickly rose through the ranks. He was paranoid, unpredictable, and ruthless. Not a good man to disagree with unless prepared to kill or die instantly. But the Pachucos themselves were afraid of him. They kept secrets. Paranoia caused him to move on. Manhattan seemed likely because the heat knew so much about him. It's a cinch to evaporate into the New York Hispanic community. Bang! Another Rodriguez or Gonzales on an apartment-house bell cluster full of 'em. New York would cover him. Just like it covered the owners of all those Chinese restaurants. Maybe he'd hire a Chinese accountant and turn his books over to IRS for a laugh.

It took some doing, but eventually Manhattan got too hot. Not police heat. The man seemed to have no time for Rafael. He'd learned from his lawyers that the New York prisons were stuffed to the max. It was hard to put a man away if they wanted to. Let alone keep him there. But Rafael had joined a gang, a crew of pirates called the Comancheros. This association brought with it some very excessive heat indeed. From the many people they ripped off.

They were in the trade the mean way. A mix of PRs, solo Mexicans, a few vagabonds from the Cuban coke trade, they were a solid army of *nasty*!

Rafael quickly showed his mettle and took the lead. A fierce gang grew fiercer still. Two berserk Pachucos from the West Coast days arrived, and Rafael employed them as his private guard.

The Comancheros would hit anyone if the cash flow was steep enough, but they specialized in bookie joints and drug retailers. They were feared and hated, and in return feared nothing that moved. Not even the Italians. At first they'd stayed clear of the Rasta ganja shops, but their unpopularity in Manhattan led them into East New York, where they began hitting the downtown Brooklyn Rasta ops. Rastafarians generally fight back, and Rafael had to be prepared to lose a man or two if he wanted to hit them. And what general is not prepared? Fact is he had too many men. As far as he could see there was no end to the spoils of terrorism. But it was hard keeping them all happy, and dangerous not to. He had a fucking army to feed.

So it was by sheer coincidence that Rafael set up headquarters near what had once been Alvira's Embryo Plaza. Wyona Street. Years ago it had been a mix of newly arrived ethnic workers and housekeepers. Now it was desolation personified, with Rafael providing the only exception to the dead stillness of urban ruins.

Around them the Rastas had their areas, as did the blacks and other Latins. But Wyona Street itself was strictly Comanchero. Even the streets directly nearby were dead, belonging to no one. No one wanted them. They offered nothing but menace and death.

There'd been no opposition when the Comancheros moved in. Moreover, they'd stepped into a virtual fortress, an embassy situation. No one would go near this turf. These were not streets on which men passed each other casually. Confrontations were the rule, like in a war zone.

Packs of wild wolfish dogs and young desperate human rat packs, swarming, hanging around in condemned buildings, turning on anything in sight. Each other.

Even JJ and Furman, who lived just a few blocks away on Miller Avenue and Dumont, hadn't gone near Wyona Street in years.

Surrounded by rooftop guards, changing buildings every

few days, keeping the area looking like it was under military occupation, Rafael was able to feel safe.

His cruelty had led him to the rank of general. He'd killed and risked death repeatedly for the spot. It was *his*!

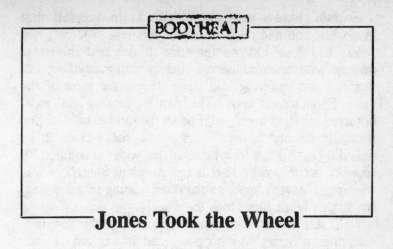

Jones Took the Wheel

Eric Shomberg parked the taxi and got out, lighting a ciggy and scanning Rivington Street through his dark RayBans. He'd booked high all day and was about to bring the yellow beast back to the garage when he decided he'd give himself a little itty-bitty treat.

He'd been tapering off lately, due to the insanities of scoring on the street. But a passenger he'd picked up earlier, a sloppy sunglassed girl in a baggy leather jacket, showed signs of the lotus in her itching eyes and slow speech. He'd started a sound on her and learned that there was some very good schmooz to be had on Riv off Bowery. Dr. Nova's old spot. No, Nova was not *the* smokin' bag at the moment. Frequent busts had driven them deeper into the Lower East Side, back to Alphabet City, although they occasionally set up a two-man crew for a few hours on Riv. But fuck Nova. Check Triad. A smoker! The girl didn't know who they were, but the bags were marked with the word *Triad* in red, or *Rainbow* in blue. Straight-up goodness! One bag should do it unless you're a pig. Eric thanked her for the sound and went on with his day.

He didn't have to get high. He hadn't turned on full-blast in a while and had no Jones at the moment. The past two weeks had been hideous for him; shitting and shivering, driving with frazzled nerves, barely doing anything but working and suffering. No sleep. Depressed most of the time. Spontaneous tears. The part of kicking that most bothered him was over, and if he let the shit be, he'd be fine soon. Be the first time in years he was really clean. If he pulled it off. All day long he struggled with the conflict. To score or not to score? That is the question. Shomberg was winning. He was almost on the ramp leading to the Brooklyn Bridge when Jones took the wheel!

Well, shit. A man has to enjoy *something* in this here life.

Rivington Street was hopping, and it was easy to see where the smoker was. A tenement building two doors down from the bodega. He walked up slowly, expecting one of the Latins lounging around to tout. No one came near. He lifted his shades and peered around. No steering, but plenty of in-out traffic. He could smell the score plain. He stopped a junkie coming out.

"Yo, B. What's the take on this place?"

The man turned an angry face on him, lips drawn down on the weight of three days' stubble, eyes dead. "You can score here. I'll bring you in for a bag."

Eric waved the man away. "That's fine. I'll take m'chances."

He walked into the dark corridor, causing eyes to peer into his. Still no touter. Then he jumped as a door creaked open, flattening himself against the wall. It was the door to the basement.

Chu peered into the darkness, saw the man against the wall, and assumed the worst. He drew his Charter Arms .38 and crouched in firing position.

Two men loitering near the stairway ducked for cover.

"Yo!" Eric let out. "Careful w'that iron. You c'n have m'money!"

Chu smiled. "Oh, I ain' rippin' j'off, B. Thought j'waz gonna rip my ass."

74

Eric was befuddled. "What?"

"J'was agains' thee wall, man. I fig' a cop o' stickup. But I seen j'face befo'. Got tracks?"

"Sure, plenty." Eric showed his arm.

"Sorry, man. C'mon in."

Eric was shaking but managed to regain his composure. He lit a cigarette and offered Chu one.

"No, thanks. How many?"

Eric bought five bags. They were stamped Triad, just like the girl said. He was about to leave when Chu apologized again.

"Listen, B, we gotta be on ou' toes. From now on yus' walk in an' rap two fast fives on thee do'."

"Sure, sorry."

"Don' eber flatten agains' thee wall." Chu turned to the loiterers. "Out a heah, assholes. Fuck w'm'customers an' j'git hurt!" He turned back to Eric. "Hey, I gib j'a hard time. Here a bee-zag on me."

Eric loosened. He exhaled smoke from his nostrils and looked at the crewman closely so he'd remember him. It was almost unheard-of for anyone to give a free bag away. On promo maybe, but not a smokin' bag.

"Thanks, man, you're all right," Eric said.

Chu put his fingers to his lips and kissed the tips, blowing the kiss to the wind. "Gooood dew in those bags, B."

"Legend has it."

"We don' got no shootin' goin' on here, bu' eff j'wanna I c'n get j'off."

"Sure," Eric said, wondering, curious.

Chu led the white junkie down to a small room at the foot of the stairs. They sat on wood fruit crates around a make-shift table. There were soda bottle tops, a bottle of water, and weepers soaking in alcohol.

Chu smiled. "I gib j'uno mo' bag. J'shoulda seen j'face when I pull m'iron, man. Shit! Sorry 'bou' da' shit!"

Eric relaxed. The guy was actually apologetic, trying to make it up to him. He opened a bag with his blade and dumped the powder into a bottle cap. He took a weeper out of the glass alcohol jar, drew in some water, and shot it into the cooker. Eric struck a match, but before he placed it to the candle he was going to cook with, the powder had broken up. He heated it anyway, out of habit.

"Man, that shit broke up nice." It was rare for street material to dissolve so clear.

"Don' need heat," Chu said.

Eric placed a piece of cotton on the spoon and drew the mix up through it. He poked around for a second, then caught a line and watched the cylinder fill with blood. He booted half the shot, then sat back and drew on his cigarette. He left the point sticking in the line, the weeper resting on his arm. He felt the warm rush instantly, and it was some mean goodness he was getting behind. Far superior to what he'd come to expect on the street. He wondered if he should push in the other half of the shot.

Extended moments later Eric completed his shot, dabbed the red dot with alcohol on cotton. Sliding down his sleeve, he began to feel the waves take hold of him. His head rolled slowly as the blankness of Nod drew near.

"Man, j'ain' been behin' no Triad bags, I c'n see. Godda gib j'some coke t'level it out."

Chu administered a massive bang of cocaine in the mainline, bringing Eric back at once.

"M'man Carlos gots coke sludge, hombre. Cook like freebase. Check'm on'a way out."

Cocaine brings an addict back from being too schmoozed. And it doesn't bring you down. Most lotus enthusiasts speedball—equal parts C and D—every chance they get.

Eric thanked Chu gratefully. On his way out he did buy coke sludge off Carlos, and he hit the street feeling smashed but in control. Fact is he hadn't been so high since 'Nam. Even the cab looked friendly as he got behind the wheel and started the engine. He put the off-duty sign on and switched on the cassette deck. Modern Jazz Quartet. He was in a B-movie as he rolled the yellow monster out onto the road.

The Triad bags seemed to glow in his pocket. Such gooood shit! So much for shaking Jones, he reflected dreamily, this time entering the ramp that led onto the Brooklyn Bridge. Jones told him not to sweat it. What's five bags one way or the other? But Jones was full of shit. Eric knew he was on the verge of addiction at all times. The five bags would just be a little blowout to a new or occasional user. With Eric's metabolism, it was enough to reestablish full addiction.

Jones said, "Well, don't worry right now. Wait an' see. Lay back an' . . . "

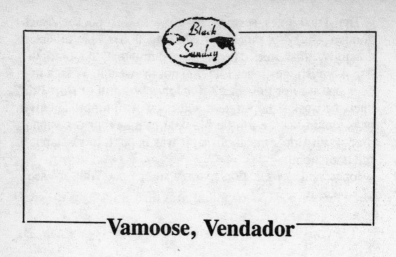

Vamoose, Vendador

A Tactical Force squad car sat outside the Dr. Nova building with four hefty peace officers in it aching to crack heads. Across Chrystie Street a blue police van was centered in the park. A display of might! Big smash.

Furman asked the cabdriver to wait a minute or two and sat back in the rear of the gypsy rig. He had to figure his next move before they made his face. He was sure the police knew faces, just from informers and hidden cameras. Too much heat here to make move one. His leather sack had the day's bundles, and his .22 was good for a year in the tank. Shit. Good day t'stay in bed.

But Furman was not easy to discourage. Sick nervous overdue junkies walked by in quivering swarms, aching for it so bad they'd rather cat-and-mouse the heat than come back later.

Too bad Furman couldn't work the bodega. That'd be best. People in and out without arousing suspicion. But the Puerto Rican who owned the store had already refused his offer of a hundred bucks a day to cover him.

"Vamoose, vendador," the man'd spat.

"The meter's on, Jack. What're you gonna do?" the gypsy driver said impatiently.

The meter read sixteen bucks. Furman threw him a twenty and a five. "Jus' relax, m'man. We gonna sit a bit."

Suddenly a flurry of activity kicked up next to the bodega. Two burly detectives came out of a building. A tall thin black man wearing jeans, a blue shirt, and a bandanna on his head was between them. It was the man from Black Mark, unwillingly on his way to the precinct.

Furman smirked. That dude had fired a few shots at him once awhile back, squabbling over turf. Still, hard to watch *anyone* in their evil hands.

The cops left, and Furman got out of the gypsy cab. He met Carlos on his way into the building.

"Que pasa?"

"Cops come bust Black Mark. Musta staked out good. Bad news. Fuckin' la hara."

Furman wondered if he should open. No touters working Black Sunday or the new Dr. Cool. If he took the shot he could sell out in a few hours flat.

An anxious blanco scuttled up. "You open?"

Other eyes were on Furman to see what he'd do.

"Yeah. Jus' walk in behin' me, man." He turned to Carlos. "I'z goin' t'work. Bring me some coffee, B."

✳

Furman sold out in two hours. A record. He sat in Carlos' kitchen at the big table, fixing, checking the street through the blinds. An old Spanish man, one of his regulars, pulled up in a battered heap and sensed heat. But he was sick, ready to take chances.

The old man walked up to one of the faces, scored, was on his way back to the car when a bearded blanco leapt out of the back of a battered van and tackled him.

Furman jumped to his feet and watched, horrified. The old man's head made a popping sound as it hit the pavement. The plainclothes who'd been in the driver's seat of

79

the van latched onto the seller as the other pulled the stunned old man to his feet, spread and searched him. He found the bags, and both customer and vendador were cuffed. The entire incident took less than two minutes. Other crewboys just stood there, frozen. Nobody had bags on them, because they all stashed in cracks and crevices until a buy came up.

One of the detectives radioed for a cruiser, and it arrived, swallowed the man and the boy. The cops glared around menacingly like bullies before getting in their van and splitting. A uniform got in the old man's now impounded heap and drove it away.

Furman felt like drawing his iron and blowing the mu-thafucka bastards to smithereens. Who in hell was that ol' man hurtin'? Jus' some poor ol' sick fuck who needed his medications t'keep from jumpin' out of his skin. Damn!

The street stayed thick with cops afterwards. Furman had to crib at Carlos'. "I ain't walkin' out there w'm'day's money, man." He called Alvira and told him he was holed up for the night.

Furman couldn't sleep later, even with an extra bang of Triad. That was rare. He usually went out at will if properly dosed on goodness. But it seemed like nothing, not all the dope in the world, could make him forget the sound of that poor old guy's head hitting the pavement. Nothing could cool the knot of hate he felt in his gut for the big well-fed blanco la hara.

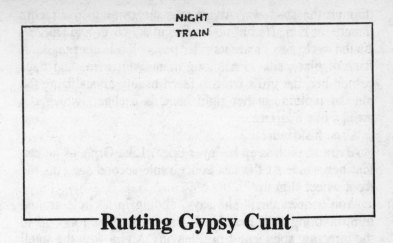

Rutting Gypsy Cunt

In a dream Alvira walks out of a modern red-brick high rise
and scans suburban streets. He is in the middle of a tall hill.
Above, the neighborhood is getting "nicer." Mansions surrounded by stone walls, a winding rustic road landscaped
into gardens. Below him is a shantytown, beyond which he
sees water. Alvira starts downward. If there's lotus around
it's down there. The waterfront. An elevated-train platform
casts shadows and threatens to crumble onto the two-lane
street that fronts the old wood docks. People are jammed
in. Blacks, Latins, Chinese, an occasional Romany face.
Alvira's eyes scan for lotus. The slow-moving apparitions
are here.

Suddenly the ground shakes.

A cluster of Mexicans roars by on stripped motorcycles.
He makes colors on the ones close to him. Ching'a'Lings.
They are dressed in black leather and sombreros, with glistening chains around their waists. They hit the corner and
fan out in all possible directions. Crackling sparks of thunder under an alien sky.

A lone rider darts ahead but then circles back. Peering

through the shadows, Alvira sees the spitting iron racing directly at him. He has no time to make cover and freezes. As the cycle gets closer its rider peels off a leather mask. A flash of black silk as her long mane whips free and flaps behind her, the girl's wolfish-faced beauty crystallizing the blur of motion. In her right hand is a chain, which she swings like a lariat.

Is she his death?

Alvira tries to keep his eyes open. Like Orpheus he can feel her wind! At the last conceivable second she cuts the front wheel slightly.

"You'll need this!" she says, sliding in a circle around him, pivoting on a long black-leather leg. She roars off in the direction she came from, leaving Alvira with the smell of burnt gasoline, roar of thunder. Down at his feet he sees the chain glinting in the moonlight. He lifts it, runs a hand along its length, ties it around his waist. Alvira realizes that he will never forget her face whisking by, the skin so tight he could see the bones beneath. Insane jet-black lotus eyes burning into him like hot liquid sparks of iron thunder.

✳

Suddenly he is standing on Dumont Avenue in East New York many years ago, where sirens wail and forecast the forbidden. Embryo Plaza! These are not streets on which people pass each other casually. Chalk of childhood and confrontation by the school yard. Red Mark on his arm. He ordered the Northern Lights and was given a pinch of powder to the wind for the souls who slipped off into Nod. Button on a peacoat pops. Sounds of distant thunder drawing near. The Robes of Forever blur around her face! A cluster of Mexicans on lean chrome and snorting iron. He stares. He will never forget them. Defying the wind. Oblivious to gravity. Colors whipping across the cityscape. Her skull before long black mane in a blur of speed. Her colors say Ching'a'Lings—Alvarado Street, L.A. The girl leaves the pack and is aimed straight at him. Eyes widen as he watches, confident that she will cut the wheel at the last second. Screech of rubber! Sound of thunder! Smell of rutting Gypsy cunt!

*

The front wheel misses him by fractions. He watches her roar off, still waving the chain. Alvira looks down at his feet. Between his boots, a small rectangular paper. He taps the folded bag with his thumb. It is transparent. There is powder inside. He knows what it is. Powdered cool. Just add water.

Alvira wakes alone with the paper in his hand. He blinks and reaches for his shades, checks the stamped logo on the bag: *Red Mark*. It is morning. He opens the bag with a small blade and lays thick lines onto a tray. As he snorts he recalls the demon girl's eyes. In them was a hunger clear as morning, real as thunder!

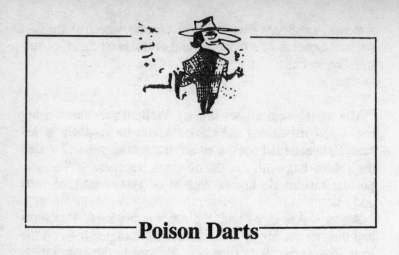

Poison Darts

The evening was moonless, fluctuating between rain and dense mist.

The stolen van approached the white T-Bird. As Rafael bent slightly to unlock the driver's door, the first dart penetrated the flesh at the back of his neck.

"That'll do it," John Jacob hissed to T. "Le's pull out!"

"Hit'm again. Make sure. Look at'm twitch, man. He don't look like a bullfighter now."

"The darts are poisoned, Tommy. No need to—"

"Once more."

JJ lifted the blowgun and aimed.

Wwwwwwwhooophh!

The dart struck deep in Rafael's shoulder. He fell to the gutter in convulsions, quivering and foaming.

"Good as dead, man. Haul it outa' heah 'fo' his people dig on us!"

"Mugs, pull this heap outa' here," T ordered. He turned to JJ. "M'lad, you've just performed a public service of the highest caliber. Hard to reward such a lofty deed. And the

84

blowgun was a stroke of genius. Silent, deadly, divine. You're an eeevil little bugger, John Jacob."

JJ beamed. "Jus' get m'black ass outa heah is reward enough."

The van slid past the Comanchero building, past the open T-Bird and its dying pilot. They made it out clean. No-body'd noticed a thing. The poison dart was instantly paralyzing, and Rafael—being alone for a change—fell right into their play.

They transferred the more conventional weapons—an M16, two pistols, a Belgian-made sniper's carbine—into the trunk of T's Jag and left the van just a block from where they stole it. No sense inconveniencing the owner.

"JJ, you're the man of the hour," T said as they piled into the Jag and settled down.

Muggles took the wheel. T and JJ spread out in the back. T took a small baggie full of beige powder out of a secret compartment.

"Now, you know I don't approve of excessive indulgence, JJ, but this is a very special occasion. We'll celebrate with this unmentionable substance. I don't encourage my close associates to fool with *shit*, but in the face of most recent events it behooves me—"

"Break it out awready, motha!" JJ shrieked. Given what he'd just accomplished, he felt a perfect right to be impatient with the Emperor.

T appeared not to notice, removing a mirror from the pocket of his gray unconstructed jacket. He slid a small wood-handled Golden Condor blade out of his boot. "Close the window, Muggles. Maybe pull over somewhere so you can get behind some of this too."

"Gotta roll, mon," Muggles said.

"Got some coke to make you roll, Dreadhead. You de-serve a nice buzz."

Muggles shrugged and pulled over. He was a little miffed at JJ for showing up with that fucking blowgun and upstaging him. But it was solid wigwork to waste the Comanchero scumbag without noisy artillery. Muggles didn't like silencers. They affected accuracy, caused malfunctions, and were at best clumsy. The blowgun was perfect, and JJ was completely proficient with it. JJ was developing a flair for tickling the Emperor.

T spilled an ungodly huge pile of the beige powder onto the center of the mirror. He broke up the tiny pebbles and granulated what had to be a half-gram of uncut. Maybe five hundred bucks' worth of happy dust.

With the delicate blade he sculpted *14-K* in one bold lightnin' line.

"Lemme clean m'chambers," JJ said. He honked into a silk hankie, then accepted a trimmed nose gimmick and vacuumed half the first number off the logo. He sat back limp on the cushy leather seat and closed his eyes. "Whewwwww . . . hold onnn." His previously adrenalized system immediately shifted into lotus.

T retrieved the tray from JJ's tilting hand. While Muggles peered out nervously, trying to cover all points, T hoofed more of the sculpture. T handed the tray to Muggles. "You're gonna have to speedball long enough to wheel us on with the night, Mugsy."

"Don' feel bad f'I an'I, bredrin," Muggles whispered, his eyes fixed on the tray. The Rasta's wide built-fo'-action nostrils gunned as he cowboyed a solid inch of Lucifer's dandruff.

T took the tray back. Most of the sculpture was still on it. "Anybody wanna go again?"

"Fuck, no!" JJ mumbled.

"I an'I pass, mon."

T slid the excess powder back into the baggie, stashed it, and materialized another baggie. "Uptown flake, Jake. Put the eyes back on Muggles' face."

Muggles hoofed a generous bump of top flake, sat back to catch his breath a moment, pulled away from the curb. T luxuriated as the Jag rolled onto the Manhattan Bridge.

Safe, surrounded by his private guard. Buddha flanked by his priests.

"Mus' pick up money, T. Drop you off?" Muggles asked.

"We'll come along." T's eyelids drooped lazily from the goodness.

They pulled up outside a reefer store on Tenth Street. Muggles bounced out and returned moments later with a paper bag stuffed with cash.

"Now T'ree Street'n C. Drop you?"

The upper echelon of Triad/Rainbow made it a rule never to step east of Avenue A. Visibility was highly undesirable in the heroin business. But T, having freshly disposed of Rafael, was in an expansive mood.

"We'll roll with ya'."

Muggles slid through junk turf until he came to the reefer op. He got out and bounced into a seemingly abandoned red-brick. He was gone a few minutes too long. T locked cash and drugs in a special safe built under the rear seat and was about to go after him with JJ. The Rasta emerged, again hefting a sack of cake. Jah be praise, mon.

T felt a sweep of utter contentment as the Jaguar roared east to the Drive. Their new Morningside Heights crib—a retreat—afforded at least geographic detachment from their professional lives. Everyone knew the narcotics business was ass-tough. Even the best had their share of ripoffs, busts, informers, murders. Uncle Satano, skeptical old fucker at first, was boggled at how well T's op was doing. When Unc's circle of dons threw highball high-vig cash at T, they got it back quickly and then some. Usually full equity took less than three days. The profit shares—large chunks of cabbage—would trickle in for another three days. More of a gush than a trickle. Since at the abstract top, all factors ever handled was cash, the risk of arrest was minimal. Very clean. With cash flow *that* high, even an arrest could be regarded as mere business expense. An unlikely one at that.

Intense cake-out brought an inherent ability to negotiate

the alleged real world effortlessly, fluidly. T felt the vibrance of it in his bones. A tingling, a taut electricity. He was picking up flashes, in his *own* presence, of the terrible magic he remembered so vividly in his father's presence.

He felt an odd flash of pity for Alvira. Too bad he had nothing to live up to. Oh, sure, he was *free*—as he always said—but would he ever achieve the insane heights T was feeling? It takes greatness of will to achieve earthly power. Greatness! Good or evil use of power is beside the fuckin' point! Power! Abstract to the goatherds! To the select few, a corporeal conquest over mortality!

Success also brought with it a strong status among high-placed buttoned members of Unc's family. T was well thought of among the Italian factors.

Tommy stopped at a pay phone to give Uncle Satano the good news about Rafael. What he got was: "Fer chrissakes, Tommy, you mighta triggered a fuckin' war. I hope you have some damn idea what you're doing!"

The Daydream

In the daydream Alvira is surrounded by moist maidens of every type, lying on a soft bed caressing buttocks and breasts with detached amusement. He knows if he keeps it up for a few hours he'll get an erection but is not sure if he chooses to focus on this. His indifference seems to feed the passions of the females, and they coo and woo fiercely as he yawns. He rests his head on firm freckled bosoms, and his feet on tender olive thighs. Suddenly he begins to get hard, but almost immediately the sweet apparitions start to fade. Then there is only one, a dark-haired slim vapor of a girl dressed in flowing red, with big dark lotus eyes that never quite look into his. She wafts over and tells him to turn over. She handles the weeper with great dexterity, pinching up a hunk of ass flesh and stabbing him painlessly. "No sting," she says. "It's like a water shot."

The girl slides between his legs and holds his prick in her fist. It is still hard, but the glow of the lotus is stronger than the sex glow.

The girl looks into his eyes. The fire returns to flesh.
Suddenly the dream is gone, leaving him with a picture.
It's a face he has never seen, except in the daydream.

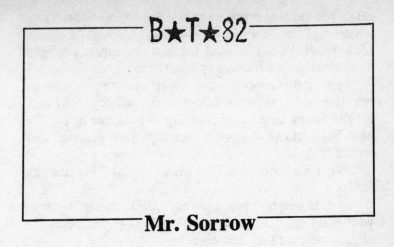

Mr. Sorrow

Furman dissolved four bags in a spoon and booted into a convenient line above the ankle, then slid on socks and boots, threw on a jacket, and hit the stairs. A quick glance at his Movado checked him at twenty minutes late. Getting out of bed was a trick with the gorilla Jones he had lately. They'd wait a half-hour maybe, but no more.

As he turned onto Dumont Avenue he saw the big dark car with JJ's impatient face in the rear window. He sprinted.

"Furman, you baaad nigga. You gonna make us blow d'day. I aks you t'be on fuckin' time, m'man. Fum now on we on'y be waitin' on you ten minutes. Sheeet!"

The problem was severe. Manhattan South and New York Tactical hit the street around eight o'clock. Between six-thirty and eight, shit was wide open. A Triad worker could sell out by noon with an early start. If the morning fucked up, it might take until seven at night to sell the day's material.

"I be sorry, JJ. Here, suck on some o' dis fine reefa an' be coo'."

"I suck on yo' reefa," JJ said, "but I don' be cooled so

easy. You be late every mornin'. It be nice o'Chu t'send wheels f'us, an' you gonna fuck it up!"

Ya Ya didn't say a word but just cut expertly through morning traffic on the way to Manhattan.

"It ain' gonna happen again. I hadda he'p m'ma w'm'kid bro'. He be fuckin' up at school again, and dey sent f'ha."

"You gonna have to tell it to Chu if it happen again. You be m'main blood, but you fuckin' up. Sho' you ain' *usin'* yo'seff blind?"

"Shit, I ain' usin' but fou' bags e'ry day," Furman said softly.

"Yo' lids weighin' in at a ton each, Jack, so don' be layin' yo' lies on me. You gonna blow one high-payin' ticket."

"Don' say dat shit. I be cool!"

"W'dat kinda usin' folks be watchin' you and you swea' dey don' see it. You think you cool, Furman. Don' trust what you thinkin'. Jones thinkin' f'you. Happnin' t' somebody else you see it plain."

Furman saw he couldn't slide around JJ and sat trying to muster the passion to respond convincingly. It was gone. Jones had it. All he could invoke was an arrangement of facial features designed to communicate amusement, innocence, detachment from allegations. But JJ's words stung into him. Furman's mouth became tight, self-conscious. The eyes made his condition totally transparent. Barely slits, lids thick, very little eye contact or looking up. Those cold vacant orbs said *Jones inside*.

"Furman, Jones makin' yo' moves. Look out!"

The car pulled to the curb beside the park on Forsythe and Rivington.

"JJ, you got 'magination up yo' fool black ass."

"M'man, you fulla shit. Yo' m'bro'n I won't be tellin' what an evil nigga you be. But ch'betta chill out o' yo' gonna fall."

Furman yanked a thin smile out of the remnants of himself. "I knows you concern. You m'*daddy*."

"You shitfucka!"

Furman stepped out, throwing the leather bag over the shoulder of his London Fog tan raincoat.

"You m'*main*," Furman said, bending to stare straight into JJ's eyes. JJ stared right back, seeing through him. Furman found himself saying, " . . . an' I ain' lookin' t'bullshit you, JJ." Furman's eyes suddenly gave up, panicking a split-second to reveal deep anxiety. "I be tryin' t'straighten shit out."

JJ exhaled in relief. Once someone admits they're out of control they might turn it around.

Furman's customers were beginning to pile up, and JJ knew he only had seconds to be convincing. "Listen, Furman, tonight we gonna sit'n rap 'bout yo' habit. Nobody gotta know. We bring it down slow, like maybe a bag less a day down to one o' half. Then you gotta take a vacation, m'man. Chu give us time to chill out upstate.

"Soun' good," Furman said, his voice exhausted, defeated. The kind of habit he'd worked up was going to be painful to break. A nutcracker.

For Furman, the worst symptoms were the mental quirks and fears, the raw nerves and eternal restlessness. Furman could contend with the trots, sweats, stomachaches, congestion, chills, nausea, and disorientation inherent in evicting the Chinaman. But the sheer hopelessness that crept into his soul scorched him bitterly. He was afraid of suicide, insanity, loss of control, of that helpless mind-set. He'd been chipping for years, once in a while going too far for comfort. But this was a *dealer's* habit. It would take something beyond courage to contend with the matter, to bear it without trembling.

"You gonna make it, Furman. You ain' alone."

"Yeah." Furman flicked his butt at the curb and put on his RayBans. "Hey, m'people're gettin' itchy t'take off."

"Sure. Go 'head."

Furman straightened up and walked into the hallway of the tenement near the bodega. The building was open, but only a few of the cribs were lived in. His spot was under the stairs, right near the rear doorway. He could split out the back or make the stairs to a maze of connected rooftops if things got nasty. And word was out on Triad, so he didn't need a touter on the street anymore. Only thing he shelled out for was the cooperation of a customer of his who lived in the building. For six bags a day, Carlos provided a small but powerful kerosene heater for Furman to huddle close to or leave at his feet to fight off the long hours. The deal also included lunch—usually hot Spanish rice, beans, and spiced fried chicken wrapped in aluminum foil and heated—and the understanding that if shit fell Carlos would be there. If it was heat, he might have to stash material— or Furman. If it was a holdup, Carlos was bound by a hand-shake to cover Furman. No contracts were signed, but the two appeared to understand each other.

Furman dealt quickly with the buildup of customers. Any cluster of blancos on Rivington Street would eventually draw heat. He set up the kerosene heater and had Carlos bring him coffee as soon as there was a break. He noticed Carlos was in a good mood and soon discovered the reason. He'd just received a substantial package of sludge. Sludge is an unshootable but very smokable yellowish-brown material similar in texture to moistened sugar. The high is similar to freebasing, a popular Hollywood and New York method of smoking cocaine. When Carlos first saw the blancos freebasing, it dawned on him that they were sort of taking the coke back a step. Since basing was relatively new, there was no commercial, ready-prepared material. Carlos hit on his contact in the Dominican Republic, who promptly opened up a line of sludge at extremely reasonable numbers. Carlos put out fives, tens, twenties, and fifties tinfoil packets of primo smokable coke with an airplane logo stamped on them, and below it the title *B–52*. Soon there were B–52s buzzing all over the street. The lotus ghosts all agreed it was the pause that refreshes. Having a hot item like that in the building helped Furman sell his own

94

hot item. A customer could score Triad and B–52 in the same spot and speedball his ass off.

Business was brisk, but Rivington Street was no breeze. Heat frequently patrolled on foot, which they rarely did in Alphabet City. No end to the harassment, and while they rarely caught anyone pants-down, their presence could tie up the game for a whole afternoon. Also, Riv was where Chu got taken by Comancheros.

Carlos returned with more El Pico, this time laced with a touch of methedrine crystal to potentialize the caffeine. He also brought Furman a banana con cuso, a thick joint of reefer and sludge. Furman needed both.

Two nervous blancos stumbled noisily into the hallway with fists full of tens. Furman threw out their bags and swept up the green.

"Mira!" It was Carlos. "La hara!"

"Yo, m'man, close 'at do'," Furman hissed to one of the blancos. The customer looked confused but obeyed.

"Ahmmmm. . . . Don' leave yet, y'all. Step down behin' d'stairs f'one sec."

Furman blew out the candle and stashed his bags in a deep gaping wall hole. His ears were cocked for Carlos' instructions because Carlos could watch the street from his window. A full five minutes stretched painfully along. They could sit there all day. The blancos were getting jittery, and Furman was about to tell them to walk a flight up, staying away from the windows facing the front, and let themselves out through a vacant rear apartment. Just then. . . .

"Esta bien!"

Furman exhaled sludge in relief, opened the door, and excommunicated the blancos. He looked up and down the street as they split. His heart was pulsing, hands sweaty. Damn thrill a minute on Rivington. The man had blown any action that might've made the place jump. Hopefully in a few minutes the customers and crews would pop out of a million different shadows and go back into action.

It took a few hours, but Furman sold his bags. He went into Carlos' crib, where he could count the cake and get off in peace. He needed that after-work cura more than usual. Maybe he'd throw an extra bag in the cooker to calm his nerves.

"Muchas gracias," Carlos said, nodding at the two bags Furman dropped on the kitchen table for him. "I hab t'go t'New Yersey toni', so I boot one an' sabe uno f'moonyana."

"Be back befo' I opens?"

"Mos' likely, 'less m'Cheby blow up."

"Well, fill the heater an' leave it under the stairs. I'll bring m'own lunch. Damn if I ain' sick'a rice an' beans nohow!" Furman grinned, challenging.

"Hey, m'fucka', don' like m'cheecken?"

"Yeah, big smash on yo' chicken, Jim."

"J'don' care 'bou' food no more w'dee dope."

"Hey, I ain't doin' that much!" His voice went into excited falsetto. "Shit, man, why're people behin' buggin' me today? I be cool, Carlos. An'f you catch m'man JJ, you be tellin'm that, too. Furman is a down nigga an' is in slick operation!"

"No'sing fool me. People come here t'buy e'ry day . . . c'n see j'slippin' away. Dey see j'get weak an' j'*fucked*, man."

Furman had been about to cook and shoot his cura when Carlos opened the superego assault on him. He looked around nervously. If he took his gimmick in the bathroom, Carlos would know exactly what he was doing. He thought of the four bags tucked in the lining of his jacket and could contain himself no further. He knew his actions would prove Carlos' words, but . . .

"If you had to stand there all day takin' chances maybe you'd be blown out yo'seff, shitface," Furman spat, pumping up his line and applying a tie.

"I takin' chances, Furman. An' I gettin' high to cool. Bu'

j'gotta put a limit, man. I ain' tellin' it no more 'cause j'don wanna hear. Foook it! Do what j'gonna do."

"I'll get a grip on it, Carlos . . . when the time's right. F'now'm unda the gun."

Furman finished fixing and split to make his cash drop. He knew people were getting disgusted with him. Somehow he'd have to chill out his gorilla.

DR. ☆ NOVA

Starlight

The park and streets were empty. El zoocho. A few venda-dors were stalking around, but no one was holding or would risk going near his stash.

Eric saw a dude he knew from Black Mark, but as he approached, the crew worker said, "Red light! Keep walkin'." The oil-drum fire used by Black Sunday was blazing away, but no workers huddled around it.

On Allen Street near the bathhouse he found out why. Star was standing there, but before he could ask her what was happening, the man approached on wheels. Metal intercom voice: "You! I'm gonna put my fist up your ass if you're not out of here in ten seconds!"

"Kinky devil," Eric said to Star, peering into the police car. Three uniforms and a detective. Shit. He and Star walked towards Delancey.

"That's Chico the Cop," Star said, "an' he don't play. That's why the street's like this. Do yourself a favor an' go home. Betta be sick at home than in jail." Star sniffled, sick herself. Her tall thin black body moved awkwardly, painfully as she walked. Jones in the bones.

"If I don't score soon'm gonna jump clear outa m'skin," Eric groaned.

Star smirked. "Got cho' wheels?"

"Aroun' the corner."

"Let's go over to Second Street. Maybe the Toilet is open."

Eric told Star to sit in the back of the taxi, and he threw the meter. Too many uniforms around to look at all unusual. He'd have to pay off the meter from his own pocket and slip Star a bee-zag for her expertise. But without her, his odds of scoring were blank.

Second Street was infested with young ambitious rookies walking in packs of four, caressing their phallic nightsticks and aching to crack heads. A cruiser sat outside the hole that was the new Triad spot. And the Toilet was not open. Everything was understandably closed.

"There's a new Triad op across the bridge, baby. Over in Brooklyn where LaTuna used to work. Got the time?"

"Don't have much choice."

"Le's go. But you gotta git me back to Rivington Street after we sco', m'man."

"Cool."

They rolled off the Manhattan Bridge onto Flatbush Avenue, turned left, penetrated one of the most forbidding mixed ghettos in the New York area. Puerto Ricans, Rastafarians, and Yankee Doodle blacks do not like to share turf. Problems tend to simmer. An outsider can smell the tension.

"Damn, Star, I ain't gonna get out of m'cab around here. These folks cook pale-eyed muthafuckas f'dinner."

Star chuckled. "Naww. White devil meat's too stringy, m'man. But cho' right 'bout dat. You ain't gitten out aroun' here. You'd be daid f'sho. This'z one time m'black ass is a *serious* social asset."

No cops visible. Perhaps they were all on the Lower East Side. Star had Eric pull up outside the old LaTuna club. The hole was boarded up. Ten feet away, another boarded-up wreck had a few cinderblocks missing from the front, and a touter hawked Triad loud and clear.

"Awri', Eric. Ah'm goin' to sco'. Wha'ch'want?"

"Bundle, Star. Get us a play."

"No promos on Triad, Eric. Good D. You be suckin' yo' toes on one bag."

A tap on the taxi window made Eric jump.

"You! Git that cab outa heah!" an angry crew worker was fuming at them.

Eric didn't move quick enough, and the guy kicked the side of the cab with his boot.

"C'mon! It's hot out hea, fucka! Git me busted I kill you, fuckin' white boy asshole!"

Eric pulled away.

"Lemme out!" Star shrieked. "Don' make me walk!"

Eric pulled across the street and let Star out after giving her an extra twenty to cop for herself. "I'll be aroun' the corner."

A stench of yen sweat permeated the taxi. Ten, twenty, thirty minutes. Damn, he was getting sicker, and things were looking evil. Like Starlight went for the easy buck and riffed him. Now he was not only sick but broke. And with close to fifteen bucks bogus on the clock. Piss and damn and shit!

Just as he was about to give up and split, he turned and saw Star walking towards him. She made the thumbs-up, and a deep feeling of relief charged through Eric's body.

"Damn, Star. Thought you got busted or taken off."

"Or maybe decided t'take *you* off?" she challenged.

Eric shrugged.

"I had to wait for the bagman to re-up. Y'know how they fuckin' stop everything an' count the cake befo' re-up. Drive y'crazy waitin' but . . . Star don't take her friends off, Eric. Now git us outa heah."

That was not entirely true. Fact was, Star made her daily Jones taking off junkies. For some reason, she'd always played straight with Eric. Maybe because he threw her a few bucks or a bag when he could and she didn't have to ask. But Eric knew that Star, like any street junkie, would take *anyone* off if she was sick enough. Desperation was part of the game, and no matter how long you did bizz with someone, if you caught them at the wrong time you'd be chumped and scumbagged for every cent you had. Just a rule of the road, a piece of the code. Nothing personal. No grudges. You were *stupid*, and the turkey that took you off selling dummies was *smart*.

Eric was too sick to drive. They parked outside a Greek luncheonette on Flatbush Avenue, and he took his bags and made the bathroom. He came out wearing a wide smile under the dark RayBans. In a good mood, he slid Star an extra bag.

They ordered coffee and pastry. Then it was her turn to commandeer the porcelain facilities.

Later, dropping her off on cop-thick Rivington, he felt a sharp sting of pain and pity while watching her walk into the desolate density of it. She had no place to go but the street, no matter how mean it might get. Since she slept and took her abbreviated meals and fixes in the park, the street was literally her home. Her indoor life consisted of infrequent visits to the bathhouse on Allen Street and occasional overnight residence in a shooting gallery. The street was her home . . . and she was always *at home*.

Suddenly he wanted to help her. She didn't deserve to suffer so. What was her crime? Being incongruous?

Eric picked up a fare and found himself inching through midtown with a harried exec and his bimbo tsking away profoundly on the back seat. The goodness gave him patience and fortitude, and his instincts guided the taxi with unflinching expertise. What could he do about Star? He was hardly in a position to help anyone do anything. Best he could do was throw her a bag when he could and not get too pissed when, inevitably, the time came for her to get sick and beat him for a few measly bags of God's goodness.

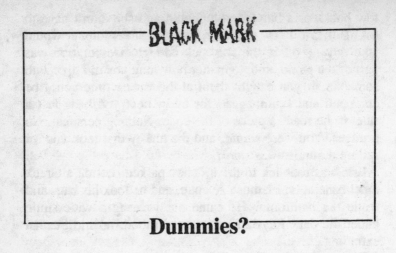

Dummies?

Furman D. Whittle sat back in the rear of the taxi and gazed out the window with lazy lotus eyes as the yellow dart swept over the Manhattan Bridge and onto downtown streets. He'd just had his morning medicino and was waking up slowly.

"Take Bowery over to Rivington," he told the driver with subdued authority.

Lately Furman rode in with JJ and they picked up together from Chu before going to work. But today was a break in routine. He'd told Chu yesterday he had to take the kid bro' to school and Moms to Welfare. Chu had arranged for Ya Ya to drop the bags on Riv so Furman could still accomplish a day's work. Chu was a good boss when it came to shit like that. He was flexible and easygoing. He had a lot of power but never used it to humiliate or crack the whip on anyone. Long as you sold your bags he was on your side. And Chu took chances, just like workers under him.

He spotted Ya Ya's wheels, which meant he could pick up

and kick in. The meter read twelve, so he dropped a twenty on the gypsy driver and went to work. The action peaked in moments. His regular customers had been waiting.

Furman stood under the stairs by his candle, switching bags for dinero frantically. Before midafternoon, he was sold out, standing on Chrystie and Riv trying to hail a cab over to his cash drop.

It was cool and windy, and Furman was anxious to get back to his Brooklyn crib. Maybe he'd have the cab wait while he made his drop, then whisk him home. But first he'd have to catch one. No gypsies worked the area. The Yellows got yellow when it came to picking up blacks. Only afraid they'd end up in Harlem or East New York. Furman tightened the silk aviator's scarf around his neck and zipped his brown leather jacket all the way up. The cold pissed him off. He was due a vacation. He dreamed about kicking his Jones in the tropics.

Furman was about to toss it in and strut when an old, rust-calico, battered MG with Jersey plates pulled up a few feet away. He recognized the driver. One of his PR customers whose name he didn't know. The guy was a steady face, buying half-bundles every other day or so.

"M'man, yo' too late. Sold out early today," Furman said, putting his scarf down just enough to uncover his mouth.

The PR was sucking a reefer and motioned for him to get in.

"Sho', B." He needed to get out of the cold. "But ain' no way I c'n sco' f'you now."

"Don' worry 'bou 'eet. I yus' wanna rap wi'j. Wanna ride somewhere?"

Furman exhaled dense reefer smoke through his nostrils as an idea popped in on him. "Tell you what, m'man. Gimme a lif' back to Brooklyn an' I throws y'all m'own cura. Two bags."

"J'got eet. Furman's j'name, B. Ri'?"

"Yeah. Yours?"

"Flaco. Leesen, man, I gotta bery cool deal f'j't'hear. J'in'rested een makey mucho dinero?"

Furman smiled. "I be makin' mucho dinero, B. But I got ears."

"I scorin' fum j'now f'months, Furman. I see j'bery slick an' down. I show j'some'sing j'swear don' tell nobody."

"Do it. No, hey, wait. Pull up an' let me take care o' somethin'. I come back an' heah you out."

"Cool."

Furman had Flaco pull up over a block away from the drop, so the guy couldn't check where he was ducking in.

Upstairs, Chu counted the cake with lightning speed, then threw Furman his take. Six hundred bucks in fifties. "Need some small bills for the taxi?"

"No, I be cool."

Furman smiled and pocketed his coin. He made more than any of the other workers because he sold more bags. He was the only Triad ready to hassle with Rivington Street. Of course Furman was afraid, just like the others, of the heat and the danger. He carried iron and hoped for the best.

When Furman returned to the MG, Flaco fired another reefer.

"Okay, man, take the Manhattan Bridge, then Flatbush Avenue to Linden and left into East New York."

"Tha'z hebby turf, Furman. I know eet. Got frien's roun'."

"So what's on yo' min', B?"

Flaco reached over and opened the tiny glove box. His fingers riffled under baggies full of reefer until he came to what he was looking for. It was a rubber stamp: *Triad*!

"Hey, where in fuck did j'git that?"

Flaco showed him a stamped piece of paper. It was a perfect copy of the Triad logo. The early mark, that is. During the first few weeks of operation, all bags were stamped *Triad*. Then one day two Chinese went to Chu and were taken to T and Alvira. The Chinks were pissed because they were real Triads. They were afraid the police would put heat on them because of T's choice of a name. To Alvira's complete amazement, T apologized and promised to use the word *Rainbow* on future bags. It evolved into *Triad/Rainbow* for a while. Then they started putting *Triad* on one side and *Rainbow Society* on the other.

"I yus' got it."

Furman felt his heart accelerate. He'd heard the gang that ripped off Chu on Rivington Street in the early days might've made off with a stamp. That was the only explanation. If Flaco was in with the Comancheros he might be setting off a bad play. Furman put his hand in his jacket pocket, slid the safety off his iron.

"What're you gonna do with it, man?"

Flaco shrugged. "I donno. Maybe make some muny. Wanna hear how?"

"Dummies?"

Flaco nodded. "Dummies, man. How'd j'know?"

Furman frowned grimly. "M'people catch you an' you daid."

Fear did not appear to be one of Flaco's concerns.

"People trust Triad 'cause the bag come stamped an' sealed. Straight from the factory. M'people work hard t'give their bag a smokin' rep. Fuck it up, Flaco, an they *got* t'waste yo' ass."

"Hmm. They no catch me, Furman. I gota heat-seal machine. Wanna sell an extra hunred bags a day? Extra grand a day, man!"

"Until they—"

"Fibe hunred each! Take thee shot!"

"Yeah, you take the shot, man. Pull this bucket up. I'z gittin' out o' heah now!"

Flaco pulled up, turned a suspicious look on Furman.

"I figure j'*down*, Furman."

"Shit! I ain't *that* down, fool. Fuck wi' Triad an' you gonna get killed. I don' wan' nothin' t'do wi'you an' yo' crazy play."

"Don' tell thee bosses, Furman. Ri'?" Flaco's eyes took on a cold glitter. A warning.

"Don' threaten me, you punked-out asshole." Furman opened the door and started getting out. "Tell y'all what, Flaco. I don' know yo' ass from shit, but what the hell, if I c'n keeps y'all from gittin' hurt . . . gimme the stamp. T'morrow I give you a bundle an' we forget—"

"No sanks."

"Shit! I'm payin' t'save yo' life! Damn chump I am. Do what you want to, Jack. Fuck yo'seff. "

Flaco's face said he was going on with his plan with or without Furman. "Change j'min', Furman, I be roun'."

"Hey, do me a solid, Jim. *Don'* be aroun'. You bad company. I ain't sellin' you no bags no mo'. Don't come on Rivington t'sco' no way from me. I be clean w'm'people, man. Dat be dat!"

Flaco smirked wide. "Scared, man. Let j'boss make thee muny an' j'get chump change f'hebby chances."

"I said fuck yo'seff *please*." Furman slammed the door and walked into the wind, eyes peeled for a gypsy cab.

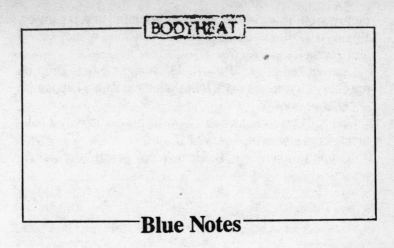

Blue Notes

The old Eldo paused on the corner of Avenue A and Sixth Street. Kathy jumped over into the back seat as JJ got in the front next to Chu. Chu resumed driving.

"I can't hab it no more, JJ. Talk t'you firs', den t'Tommy an' Alvira."

"I 'preciate dat."

"J'gotto sound him right! Furman fuckin' up bad, an' eet look bad f'me, B. All of a sudden las' few days he makin' his drops like he sleepwalkin'."

"I did sound him, Chu. Furman be a thick fucka, specially when it come t'his Jones. He be layin' a bad numba on hisseff. All dat cake slidin' through his fingas. He helpin' his family, man. His little bro' be a winna. Bu' must be a bad gorilla he ridin' now, 'cause no matta how much he make, it gone."

"Furman j'hombre, JJ. Tha's what got him into Triad. He owe it t'j't'straight it out!"

"I'm gonna lay it on him again."

"J'don' wanna blow shit w'Triad."

"No way, man. No complaints. I neva live so high. Be

puttin' cake in a deposit e'ry day. Helpin' m'folks git by. Buyin' new vines alla time. Y'all been solid w'me, Chu. I ain' gonna let m'man down."

Chu winked at JJ. "J'awri', JJ. Straight it out. Drop on me ebery day 'til we work it out'n tell me wha'z happnin'."

"That be cool."

Chu had driven in a circle. Now he pulled up only a half-block from where he'd picked JJ up.

"Git on Furman *now*, B. He awready pushin' our luck."

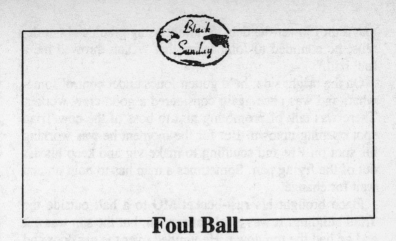

Foul Ball

Furman's luck went from bad to deplorable. An attempted recovery from economic pressures got him in deeper, and he was feeling the twist. The number was a reefer run. Furman put up twenty grand—half the cake necessary to load up a car trunk with private-garden California green. Some of the cash was from his emergency stash, but most of it was borrowed from a couple of black shylocks. Tig promised to hold down the vig if Furman cut him in nice. He also made it clear that if anything went wrong he did not want to be cut in on the loss. Furman's ass was one hundred percent on the line. The risk factor sat entirely on his head.

In Furman's haste, this seemed agreeable. He crossed his fingers and rented the car, hired a trusted driver, arranged to warehouse and distribute the product, and prayed for Allah's assistance.

On the way back from Calif the vehicle was spot-checked by highway patrol. The driver took a fall. The car and contents were confiscated. Furman had to borrow five grand from a third shylock to make bail on the driver so he wouldn't inform. Vig alone was a few grand weekly, and that didn't lower the debt. Without being graphic about details, he confided to John Jacob that "Allah threw me a foul ball."

On the bright side, he'd gotten Jones under control somewhat, and was once again considered a good crew worker. There was talk of promoting him to boss of the new Triad spot opening uptown. But for the moment he was working his spot on Riv and scuffling to make vig and keep his ass out of the frying pan. Sometimes a man has to hold on and wait for change.

Flaco brought his rust-bucket MG to a halt outside the Triad building. It was a cold afternoon, but the sun was out and he had the top down. He jumped over the car door and bopped to Dr. Nova, which was a few feet away. Jabber jabber. Finally he detached himself from the crew huddled around the oil-drum fire and walked into Triad.

"Furman, m'man! How j'doin'?"

"Buy yo' bags'n split, Flaco. I'm a busy man."

"Gimme fi' bags."

Furman counted bags into Flaco's open palm and took the crisp new fifty.

"So j'still don' wanna makey muny?"

"Nope. Git lost."

"Thick-headed fool. Yus' uno dummy in ebery bundle an' j'makin' extra fibe hunred a day."

"I pass."

"Be coo', B."

As Flaco got back in his car he heard his name. He turned. It was Furman. Flaco went back under the stairs.

"Wha'z up, Furman?"

"I need mo' bucks, Flaco. Bring me some dummies tomorrow. We see what happen."

Flaco smiled. "Why wait 'til moonyana. Be ri' back." He chicken-bopped back to his short, lifted the boot and extracted a small package, bopped back to Furman.

Prepared dummies.

Furman held one up to a Triad bag. They were indistinguishable. "We give it a shot, Flaco. Jus' keep yo' face shut tight."

"M'man, I don' wan' no fuckin' body t'know either."

Furman frowned. It was a bad idea whose time had come.

"Anybody breeng eet up, say sometime dee powder ain' mix," Flaco suggested helpfully.

"Flaco, I don' like to be doin' this shit a'tall, an' you is a smelly bag o'douche in my opinion. We straight on 'at shit?"

Flaco smiled broadly. "I 'preciate j'honesty, hombre."

"Cool. Now split."

"Gimme fi' more Triad, Furman."

Furman counted out five, held out his hand for cake.

Flaco slipped him skin instead. "Yus' write me down f'fibe. Settle when j'pay me off."

Furman flinched, realizing instantly the ramifications of Flaco's game. No one to blame now but himself. "Five bags, Flaco. I gonna write it down."

Flaco smiled. "Bes' t'write down a transaction between partners."

"Yeah. Sure. Zit-faced twerp. Split row!"

Flaco turned gracefully and walked out of the stairwell. He rapped on Carlos' door and bought some coke sludge before chicken-strutting triumphantly back to his MG.

Furman took off his boot and wiggled his toes in front of the heater. His socks were soaking wet, and he concentrated on drying them. Sanity depended on not thinking about what he had just done.

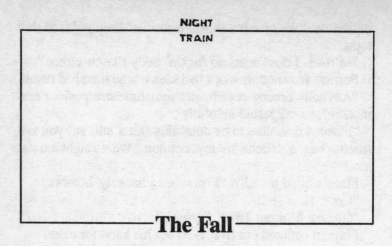

The Fall

Furman was making his vig and then some, but Jones crawled right up on his back and sat there triumphant, an unshakable entity determined to call at least some of the shots. With all the pressure on him lately, relapse was inevitable. He was closing high, as if to make up for clean time. Oddly, working comforted him lately. Since the shylocks were unlikely to go near junk turf, it was the only place he felt safe. Furman traded his small pistol for a .38 and hoped for the best.

A few weeks of passing dummies slid by more or less without incident. People occasionally complained, but as Flaco predicted, he lost few customers. Even with one beat bag in a bundle, Triad was a better buy than anything else.

The dummy cash went to paying vig and principal on his debts. Yet all problems appeared trivial if he tried to short-count Jones. The monkey kicked him in the nerves, where it hurt!

The day started heavy and stayed that way, customers not giving his ass a chance to breathe. He didn't have time to place dummies in the bundles. Close to six o'clock and he hadn't passed one dummy yet. Shit. Couldn't afford to lose the cake. It was already spent.

Soon there was a break in action. Furman was about to start placing dummies when he realized he was almost sold out of real bags. Fuck! It was Friday, and he was just a few bags away from calling it a day.

A white girl stumbled in sleepily dazed and wanted two bundles. He recognized her as an occasional customer and almost told her he was selling out. He stopped himself with a terrible thought.

"Lemme see'f I c'n help you, sis. Jus' do me a favor an' walk out the door. See if the man is on the street. I be right out w'yo' bags."

The girl looked slightly suspicious, but Triad had the best rep around. She did what she was told, saying, "You should throw me a play for watchin' your back," as she walked out.

Furman smirked. Everyone tried to hustle his poor ass. Triad/Rainbow don't do no play. Bes' bag around. They can't be expected to give'm away. The girl's attempt to wiggle an extra bag out of him put an end to his hesitation about beating her. He put a rubber band around a beat bundle. Irony caused him to take a real Triad out of his pocket and add it to the package. Sure . . . he'd give her a play for keeping lookout two minutes.

"Heah y'go, sugah," Furman said. "You got ch'play. Now take off an' lay." He pocketed her cash.

"Hey, thanks, m'man," Sleepy Eyes said, almost brightening.

Her sniffling junk-sick mannerisms made him nervous. He watched through inebriated eyes as she walked away. Hell.

Furman had never done anything nearly as nasty on the street. But shit, people tried to hustle him all the time, and he needed those bucks now. She was just a junkie cunt. Just have to trick some more money and try again. What the fuck could she do about it?

Layin' beat powder on people was not his style . . . but

damn, Jim. The show must go on. Havin' some dumb shylock blow his ass away was a lot worse for business than offing a beat bundle on some white trash.

The Horror

Monday morning started with a bang . . . of *speedball*. Equal parts cocaine and dope gave Furman the kind of wake-up charge Farmer Gray got out of bacon, pancakes, and poontang. He met JJ and Ya Ya on time and rode into Manhattan feeling fine on cloud nine.

The weekend had gone well. Furman was up on his vig thanks to a lucky poker hand staked by none other than Flaco's beat bags. He didn't feel good about it but. . . .

The action began at once and continued until just after three o'clock, when he took a break. He sat down close to Carlos' heater and slid dummies into the remaining bundles.

Around five Flaco dropped by to cop and pick up his cash. Furman attempted to act friendly, but he couldn't help feeling that Flaco was a worthless slum rodent. His association with Flaco was contemptible, but Flaco was helping him at the moment. He had to be cool. Since he was cooperating, it would not be wise to piss the dude off. He paid him off in cash and real Triad bags and took the next day's dummies.

Furman sold out by six. He stepped into Carlos' crib for a cup of El Pico and to count the day's cash. Alvira was easygoing about trivia, but T made a big stink if the cake wasn't wrapped in thousands with each bill facing the same way. T and Alvira had a bank-style counting machine in their office. Once or twice a week it went full blast twenty-four hours.

Carlos was frying pork chops on the stove and offered Furman a bite. But Furman's appetite was for dope. He booted two before packing the cash in his leather case, putting on his jacket, and hitting the street. He felt loose and light.

Furman's attention was on an approaching taxi, but he caught a glimpse of motion out of the corner of his eye and turned to check it out. On the street motion *is* menace. There was no time to duck or make cover, or even flinch.

Whommmp!!

The baseball bat descended, clipping his ear and hitting with full impact on his right shoulder. He was stunned, hand frozen inches from his iron. The attacker was wearing a black ski mask and leather jacket. He was big, powerful, determined to brain Furman with his bat.

Seeing the heavy wood being lifted over him, Furman recovered his animation instinctively. He moved as the bat came down. It hit the brick wall behind him. Furman stumbled, trying to sidestep the man. Another man stood on his other side, unnoticed. Furman whipped out iron, but too late.

Whommmp!!

The bat came down forcefully, full on Furman's skull, making a hollow cracking bone sound and causing him to bite through his tongue. He howled with pain, falling to the pavement in front of the Triad building. Blood trickled from his eyes and ran freely from his mouth.

Carlos came running out with a kitchen knife but was met with a baseball bat across the eyes. He stumbled over Furman's quivering body and fell on his face. A bat was shoved in Carlos' groin.

"Snooky! He's down!"

Furman was glazed over but not unconscious. He forced himself to his feet. The gun had fallen out of his hand. Shit! And he'd dropped the leather bag with the day's cake. His clouded eyes fell on the approaching form of a girl.

All he could make out was an outline as she came from between parked cars. He could see that she had a car aerial in one hand and a bottle or jar in the other. He tried to back up and press himself against the red-brick wall. As she drew in for the kill he made her face. It was the white bitch he laid the beat bundle on!

"You fuckin' black bastard!" she spat. The aerial cracked across his legs, bringing him back down to pavement. He squirmed a few feet, but she kept coming. Her impassive lotus face was now twisted with venomous rage.

"This is f'you!" she hissed, lifting her arm and casting the gray coarse grainy contents of the jar in his face.

"*Yeeeeowwwwwww!*"

He clutched his face and fell over. No amount of heroin could counter the agony that shot through his twitching body as the eyes caught fire, the skin boiled. The lye burned into his face mercilessly, with a disgusting hissing and chemical smell.

The girl stood above him, grinning. She drove the toe of her boot into his balls, then another kick to the base of his spine. When she was sure he wouldn't get up, she signaled for her accomplices, and together they began walking slowly away from the squirming vendador.

Almost as an afterthought one of the men stooped and picked up the leather bag. They got into an old beat-up American long iron double-parked at the curb.

A few guys from Nova had been hanging around, but nobody stepped in. So sudden and unexpected. All over before anyone could make a move. Or want to. The crews

117

did compete with each other. If Triad closed for the day, Nova would sell out quicker.

A Nova worker went into the bodega and called an ambulance. Carlos was unconscious, but Furman sat on the fender of a car. He was clutching his eyes, in deep shock. Someone tried to put water on his face, but he screamed.

An ambulance came, and two attendants managed to get Carlos and Furman inside. The sirens wailed, then got fainter.

A moment later the street was jumpin' again.

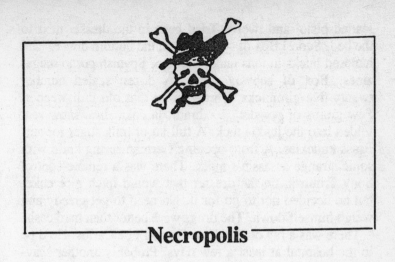

Necropolis

The young junkie's eyes were old, sagacious, torn by the life. He sat under the stairwell of the Triad op on Rivington, opening up the two bags he'd found stashed in a crack.

Furman wouldn't be needing them now. He thought about popping the lock on Carlos' door and scooping up coke sludge and anything else that might be there. Maybe some more Triad bags.

Tico drew the liquid into his gimmick and made the line on first try. It was an old weeper, and the dull point stung like the sting of an insect. Seconds later that familiar warmth was traveling up his spine, through the belly, soothing his mind like the touch of a tender lover. Instantly the hunger subsided.

Tico didn't have to pop any lock. The door swung open at his touch. He locked it behind him and went to work. Dime bags of coke sludge sat piled on the kitchen table. Hundreds of them! While looking for a big bag to put them in, he found four pounds of reefer under the sink. He jammed everything into a huge garbage bag, then continued to search. Carlos was an industrious m'fucka. There were a

loaded pistol and twelve Triad bags in the dresser next to
the bed. Score! Box of .38 ammo in the bottom drawer. Six
hundred bucks in tens under a pile of Spanish porno maga-
zines. Box of subway slugs. A dozen sealed number
twenty-five gimmicks. Throw away that old dull weeper.
Few grams of powder . . . hmm, la coka, in a snow seal
folded into the junkie tuck. A full jar of milk sugar for cut.
Brass knuckles. A front-opening German spring knife with
some strange assassin's mark. There was a remote-control
Sony Trinitron on the dresser that would fetch nice cake,
but he decided not to go for it. No need to get greedy and
weigh himself down. The drugs were better than hard cash.

There was a rap on the door. Couldn't be Carlos. He'd be
in the hospital at least a few days. Probably another scav-
enger smelling the score. Tico hefted the plastic garbage
bag onto his skinny shoulder. A pistol was in his jacket
pocket, just in case. He raised the rear window and slid out
as the front door burst open.

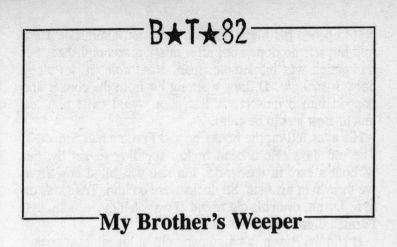

My Brother's Weeper

John Jacob Pennington sat in the dark grimy bowels of the coal bin in Brooklyn, chalk of childhood on the dim walls, smell of early mischief. He drew nervously on a fat reefer, eyeing his Mickey Mouse every few minutes. Diddly-damn! The nigga's always late! JJ'd arranged for Furman to be picked up at his crib and driven to the old coal bin. What was happening? What was keeping his ass?

'Z'if this business wasn't messy enough.

JJ did not want to execute Furman, even though the rewards would be dazzling. But Furman had betrayed Triad, and it was JJ who had brought him into the circle. T saw it as JJ's responsibility. He had to display loyalty now or step away from the picture.

JJ's nerves were unsteady as he looked around the old familiar basement bin. This was where things started for them—he remembered Chu's visit when recruiting them for Triad—and for Furman, this cold dingy coal bin was where it had to end . . . tonight. Don't the fool know he threw his cards that way? Nobody else. Throw'd hisseff an ace o' spades.

He opened his flight bag and extracted gimmicks. He'd told himself no dope until after mission accomplished, but this action was intolerable, man. Hard *doin'* it, let alone doin' it *straight*. JJ drew a strong hit from the cooker and popped into a muscle. A line shot would twist him too much. Best just to be calm.

His eyes fell on the books he and Furman had collected. The old days. He'd been broke, scuffling to get by, but without a care in the world. Furman was blind now from lye thrown in his face. Shylocks were on him, Triad was on him. Damn, even his old friend JJ was on him . . . although Furman didn't know that yet.

JJ slid the Raven .25 automatic out of his raincoat pocket and pulled back the slide, causing a round to click into the chamber. He pulled out the clip and inserted another round, then wiped off a touch of excess oil with a small chamois. With one in the chamber he had seven shots. Two or three for Furman, the rest for getting away. It was more than likely, given the neighborhood, that no one would interfere with his exit. Few honest citizens, and a complete absence of police for miles in any direction. Shadows, mostly, inhabited the dank arteries of East New York.

JJ peered out of a tiny basement window, breathless as he waited. A half-hour crept by before he saw Ya Ya's car pull across the alley. Ya Ya helped Furman out of the back seat. Furman's black raincoat looked like a cloak of doom. Enveloped in this dismal drape his old friend looked bony and unstable as he hobbled behind his cane, eyes covered by dense, almost black sunglasses, mouth tight and drawn permanently down. Furman was a young man but not a kid anymore.

Ya Ya led him down into the recesses, sat him beside JJ.

"Furman, man, I'm heah."

"JJ?" he let out tentatively. Furman sat perched against a cold cement wall, back rigid, hands on his cane. "Wish I could see y'all, JJ."

JJ laughed. "Shit, Furman, I ain't lookin' so hot now anyways."

"Oh? Got problems?" Furman grinned, the scar tissue on his face distorting his expression hideously.

"Man, Furman, you got m'ass in a lot o' trouble, dig? It's a wonda I ain't mad at you. Passin' dummies a nasty—"

"Aww, man, I fuck up, JJ. I was jus' tryin' t'stay high, m'man."

"I know, Furman—"

"F'I'z born a gennelman I'da been a fuckin' *saint*. Shit wen' wrong f'me. M'Jones got so nasty. You don' have t'tell me what a fool . . . I be sorry you got trouble fum me."

"Furman, listen. . . ." JJ held the cocked automatic in his hand, aiming it at the blind junkie.

"Wha'z'at, JJ?"

JJ's hand was on the trigger, but he couldn't squeeze. A full thirty seconds before he forced himself to squeeze the trigger. Nothing happened. The safety was on. JJ put the iron down. Fuck it! He broke open a disposable weeper. "Furman, m'main man, 'm gonna rap hard with y'all, but first'm gonna give you some *goodness*."

"Gonna get me real high, JJ?" Furman's voice was soft and crackly, like something that came from way beneath the distorted surface. His cheek twitched slightly and he breathed laboriously. The bones were set blank except for a tiny bittersweet smile that froze JJ out because it suggested that to Furman life was already becoming a distant memory, a detached reflection. Furman coughed into his fist.

"Make yo' play." His voice was husky, imploring.

Does he know? Does he realize what's shakin' here?

"Gonna git you high as you ever been, Furman."

"Gooood, B. I been sufferin', m'main. Not jus' m'face . . . m'eyes . . . I mean *inside* where you cain't see even if you got eyes. . . . I feelin' terrible bad." Furman almost choked on his effort. He ripped a sleeve open. "So hit me

123

good, JJ. I don' wanna feel nothin' no mo'. Make fuckin' sho' you hit a *line*." He was begging now, proffering his arm. "*Make yo' play*."

"I gotta aks you somethin' first, Furman."

"Wazzat?"

"Who's wigwork was passin' dummies?"

Furman winced at that awful word. He flinched and exhaled in resignation. There was no end to it. "Oh, man, some foo'. I hope de fucka choke on a bone. His name be Flaco. Donno where he from. Drive an ol' MG."

JJ knew him. Before leaving town he'd settle that score. JJ hadn't planned this, but . . . he dropped a tenth-gram of pure heroin into his cooker, dissolved it in water, placed a cotton. He drew liquid up into the weeper and accomplished a register on the first try. As he began to plunge he heard Furman moan.

"Lord, that *is* some dope you got there, JJ!"

"That's only half the cylinder, m'man."

"Half?" Furman's lids drooped, shoulders rounding as he slumped. "M'be betta jus' stop, JJ. F'get the otha' half'a this shot." He exhaled, head loose on a roll, voice husky. "Aww . . . what the fuck. . . . *Make yo' play!*"

JJ plunged the other half and looked at his watch. He knew within minutes Furman would be a cool blue corpse.

"Go with it, Furman. Jus' let it take you where it's gonna take you."

"Yeah . . . away." His limp body sagged. The skin glistened with cold sweat, eyes shut. A hand moving slowly to scratch his nose never made it and dropped onto his lap.

JJ eased him into a reclining position. This was the only merciful way to handle it, but the mess was not over. His instructions from Tommy were to shoot Furman. That would have to be done. Nobody need know that he gave him a hotshot first, that as Furman slipped into the beyond his head was all regal with lotus.

The lips popped open, dry, purplish, imperceptibly inhaling. The lids were parted, eyes rolled up white. His muscle tone approached a realm of relaxation that negated all effort.

"Furman, you'z a pile o' mush, B. You hea' me?"

"Shhh . . . JJ. Y'shrinkin' m'haid. Talkin' loud like whitey."

"Furman! You still heah, man? Feelin' fine?"

"Oh, real real fine." The words were an incoherent mumble . . . the last few words he said.

JJ checked the chamber. He'd seen enough bullets in his life, but knowing this one would soon be in Furman's head made him look at it close. Hard to tell what's comin' at a man next . . . what he might have to do . . . what he will actually do compared to what he tells himself.

JJ got up close. Furman was either dead or so close it didn't matter. JJ held the pistol steady in two hands and fired almost point-blank into Furman's forehead.

The body jerked for a flash, then resumed complete slump. For a short iron that Raven sho' spit spark and thunder. T had specified precisely how 14-K assassinations were to take place. This one might make the papers. Best to stick with what had been prescribed.

Blam!

The second bullet went through Furman's throat. The sound of dripping blood was the first thing JJ heard when the ringing in his ears stopped.

JJ wanted to prop the corpse into a more comfortable position, but he had to be movin' on. No resistance. The sound of gunfire was not enough to alarm anyone. He thought of ditching the Raven, but it felt good in his hand. Save it for Flaco.

He walked casually over to the old shoe factory, outside of which sat Ya Ya's car. The tune "Swing Low, Sweet Chariot" was in his head as he got in the back seat and told Ya Ya to roll it over to T's crib. JJ looked blankly out the window as the car slid along. He'd never forget Furman's muffled, agonized voice. *Make yo' play*. . . .

Tommy shook JJ's hand firmly and beamed. "John Jacob,

you've shown unflinching allegiance to your Triad brothers. If we were all ginzos you'd be a *made man*, a *buttoned* membrane . . . ahh, member. But I ain't no fake Pope, and this is *now*! You are the first of a special Triad force. The 14-K is your baby. You're a boss now. On salary. Three grand a week. No street time. No handling material. If you need something, see me directly. Inside the 14-K all things are possible."

JJ nodded silently. That was heady! His wildest dreams were materializing.

"First thing, JJ, get your ass out of the East Coast for a month. Way the cops've been, there just might be an investigation." He handed JJ a thick manila envelope. "Thirty grand for the road. Just don't go start a banana republic somewhere and forget to come back. I need you, JJ."

"Can't go anywhere yet."

"What? What's wrong?"

"Flaco."

"Who the fuck is Flaco?"

"The wig behind Furman's dummies. Ah'm gonna nail'm an' then split."

T exhaled. The matter was just a complication, of no importance. Unless it was a dramatic hit and strengthened the legend of the 14-K.

"Ah'm gonna give half this cake to Furman's mom, go nail Flaco, an' split."

"JJ, you're too much. Hold your cake. I'll drop fifteen grand on Furman's mother. As for Flaco, he could be Comanchero. We did lose a Triad rubber stamp when they hit Chu on Rivington Street. Those schmucks were weakened when they lost Rafael, but they're still a force to be—"

"I don' care who the fuck he is."

Tommy shrugged. "Nail the scumbag. Be swift. Murder's against the law, JJ. But do it on the street if you can. I want people to see what happens when they fuck with us."

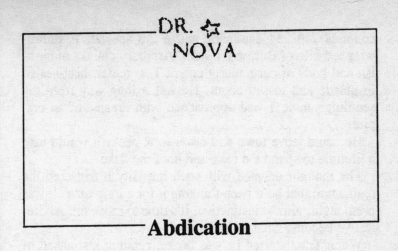

DR. ☆ NOVA

Abdication

Alvira closed the door to the tiny private room and opened his safety-deposit box. Encased in a tomblike vault beneath the turmoil and human traffic of the Necropolis, he opened a large tucked-and-folded piece of paper marked "#4." He tapped a pile of fine beige powder—the shake—into another, smaller paper, which he put in his pocket. He snorted two lines of heroin. Instant loosening of the skeleton as the metal drip hit the back of his throat. Alvira needed to step back. Furman's death sat heavy on his soul.

Alvira closed his eyes for the journey home. He'd been dosing only lightly during the Triad regime. His tolerance was down, susceptibility high. He wore stereo Walkman earphones with volume low and heard as he snorted, "Every need has an eagle to feed." "Pimper's Paradise" by Bob Marley.

Alvira felt hooked up with the essentials as his head rolled loose in Nod. He gave himself time to adjust to being so high, then peeked at the contents of his box. Over a pound of heroin, consisting of quarter-pound tastes from their best purchases. Envelopes stuffed with cash, not easily countable. A .25 automatic and a .38 special. A tinfoil-wrapped kilo of Burmese opium. Arbitrary chunks of hash-ish and buds of particularly potent Thai reefer, heat-sealed in plastic and tossed about. He was a long way from the scuffling junkie T had approached with dreams of an empire.

He could leave town and never look back. It would take a lifetime to spend the cake and hoof the flake.

The thought dawned with such intensity it triggered the realization that he'd been thinking it for a long time. It was prethought, almost instinctive. It's time to move on, Alvira, lest ye become what ye hate most!

When Triad started he was broke, running just ahead of his habit, scuffling like mad. T arranged everything. Alvira just had to agree to participate. He needed cash and to prove something to himself. No regrets. The Triad put him in a position where he could glide out on envelopes swollen with hundreds and fifties.

Miraculously nothing definitive had gone wrong . . . yet. Alvira had never trusted the future. He tried to employ in-tuition and project his future. In this sterile and unlikely cubicle Alvira abstracted into a series of head-rolling nods. The pictures came. The pictures had nothing to do with thought, in the conventional sense. And yet . . .

He bent over mechanically to snort a line of cocaine. Bring him back a touch.

His decision was somehow sealed during these chemical meditations. He was *leaving*. Now!

Furman's execution soured the aesthetic of Triad in his mind. The whole incident inflated Tommy's enthusiasm and deflated Alvira's symmetrically. Tommy saw himself as the manifestation of power. To Alvira, Triad was no longer a romantic flame burning against the winds of probability. Furman's hit marked a new era. The 14-K, Tommy called it. The Emperor's hit squad. Now they were feared above all else. Blood had been added to the Triad legend. Alvira didn't like that. Fear made people lie. Before, when people acted like they respected him, Alvira believed they did. He paid the crews well, stood by his players, sold righteous material. All of his associates got a fair shake or better. It came back at him almost unanimously. Triad had been known for straight shooting and fairness. Now that they were feared he could not trust how people treated him.

The fact that T thrived on fear put distance between them. Insoluble and fixed. Time to move on. . . .

He never went for the secret society stuff anyway. Too much like a government. It was sure to end up victimizing the very people it was supposed to serve and protect.

And why gentrify executives? Cooler to indulge gratifications and pleasures privately . . . in the empire of shadows Alvira knew so well. Maybe that was the prob. . . . Tommy never knew the shadows. He was a hotshot from *go*. Nobility by birth. Even in the can he was a heavy dude. On the street he was . . . well, Satano's nephew. Not a button, but a very well-connected man with proximity to and an ability to influence some very highly placed wise guys.

That power thing sure sets you up for strange operational and organizational necessities.

Alvira tapped the paper in his jacket pocket. Now, goodness could be hard to survive, sure. If you're lookin' to lose, the lotus will help. Like the racetrack or booze or ineffective business techniques. But if you're not lookin' to lose and have a supply, you can manage things. Not as many outside forces working against you. Using sets you up for risks—an o.d. or bust—but no one is looking to kill or replace you. If you're careful you can age gracefully on the goodness.

No kick is safe, but if the menu reads lotus or power, lotus has to win.

Alvira began emptying the vault box into his leather bag. Money, drugs, guns. Simple things for a simple life. Now that his mind was made up it would be madness to delay. Might not make it.

Alvira locked his bag in the boot of the old Triumph. No

stops to make. No pieces of other lifetimes like childhood chalk on the factory wall. He had no destination, but Alvira never feared open-ended transitions. It was inevitability he feared. And boredom, and mundane inertia.

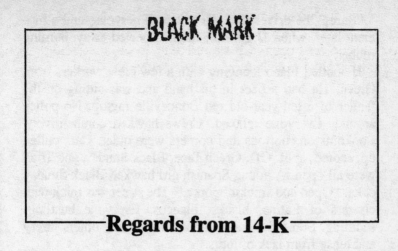

Regards from 14-K

Tommy said it had to be done on the street. As many people as possible should see it close up. Let'm smell it and taste it. Maybe get blood on'm. JJ was the sacred breath of the Emperor and must act with appropriate dignity and precision.

JJ didn't pick up on this cool crisp Monday morning. His days of selling bags were over. So with the self-evident authority of Tommy Sparks, JJ focused on his mission. . . . He was a bullet aimed at the enemy of his Triad brothers.

One thing was sure, fixed, fated. Furman was *blood*, and now the street would be splashed again with red tears. Before the sun set on arteries and conduits of Nightfire, Flaco would be the cold victim of a 14-K play.

JJ made the yellow checker pull over on the corner of Eighth Street and Avenue D. Flaco's short was parked in front of the Green Tape basement. JJ could see the hack was jumpy, so he slid a fifty through the bullet-proof partition.

"Keep the change, m'man," he said. The meter read under twenty. "But'm gonna aks y'all t'sit heah five minutes. Cool?"

"Sure," the driver said. He was still nervous, and a moment later, when JJ got out, the taxi peeled away, burning rubber.

JJ spotted Flaco lounging with a few crew workers from Green. He had a beer in his hand and was sitting on the fender of a ten-year-old red Bonneville ragtop. No police around. Everyone relaxed. Crews hawked competitively. Lookouts on rooftops and corners were quiet. Cars pulled up, scored, split. OD, Green Tape, Black Sunday, and Triad were all open. A young Spanish girl hawked Black Sunday coke. "Open and smokin' poppa!" The street was thick with clusters of Latins, blacks, blancos. Everyone hustling, scuffling. Some fluid and smooth from lotus, others jittery and tense from lack of lotus.

Perfect. Let their eyes bulge and their ears ring!

JJ wore a tan raincoat, black jeans, sneakers, a white sailor's cap, brim down. In one pocket he had the standard Triad iron: a Raven .25 auto. Kept clean and dry, it was a reliable little bugger. A round was chambered. He slid off the safety.

No one made his face yet. Time to move. . . .

JJ nodded to Domino, the Triad worker, as he started west on Eighth Street. He approached from behind, so before Flaco saw him he was a few feet away.

JJ removed a lit cigarette from his lips and flicked it at his target. A shower of sparks exploded on Flaco's shirt.

"What the fuck—"

"Go f'yo' piece, m'fucka!"

Flaco's face tightened with fear as the workers moved away. This was none of their business, and they were glad. All eyes were on them. Domino stepped closer in case JJ needed backup.

"I don' hab no piece, señor, please."

"Tha's too bad, Flaco. A scumbag like yo'seff should always have a piece."

"What I do t'jou?" Flaco tried to muster indignation. His eyes darted around. There was no cover, no time, no hope.

"This is f'm'main man Furman. Gooooodbye, fucka!"

The Raven sparked twice in JJ's hand. One hole between the eyes, one in the throat. The mark of the 14-K.

The quivering body slumped down on a car fender, slid to the pavement in a pool of bright red blood. JJ kicked the corpse over on its back. Big dumb eyes stared up at the curious.

A blanco girl shrieked in horror. No one else made a sound.

JJ slid the iron in his pocket and lit a cigarette. As dangerous as his situation was at the moment, he felt good . . . safe . . . removed.

"Ba hondo!"

"Agua! Ba hondo! Fao! Fao!"

In a moment the street would flood with sirens. JJ walked slowly towards Avenue D, the crowd parting for him. A bus waited for the light across the street. He forced himself to stand perfectly still. When the bus crossed, he got on.

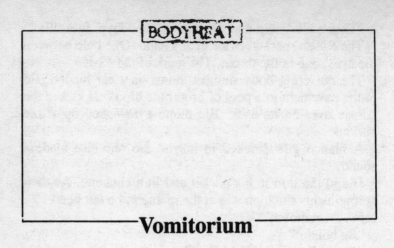

Vomitorium

The police are full of surprises. Suddenly they got serious. Heat came down in a wild sweeping flurry of bad news. A punkish white girl scored a bundle from Triad on Rivington Street. She returned an hour later for more, paid in marked cash. Two thick blancos popped out of a taxi and made the bust.

Simultaneously, four undercovers rushed the hole—the Triad spot on Fourth and C. They arrested two crew workers and confiscated hundreds of bags and twenty thousand in cash. As Saturday nights went, this one was for shitski. Things in Brooklyn were just as bad. The building Triad used to sort cash and material was surrounded and penetrated by detectives. Chu was inside, as were a dozen workers. Not a shot was fired, but they were all busted. Two kilos of unbagged number four, over one-point-five million in cash, cutting and bagging equipment, worst of all some paperwork—all confiscated. The paperwork recorded cash flow between Triad and Uncle Satano's people. The records were coded, but the numbers were high and would trigger intense investigation. Beaucoup shit!

"Red light" and "Fao!" rang like bells of doom through arteries and conduits.

On Eighth Street and Avenue D the police sweep was more visible and not as concentrated on Triad. They hit Green Tape first.

JJ—just returned from his vacation—was by checking on the new bagman when the heat arrived. They were working the foyer of an abandoned building. The detectives barged in, shotgun first. JJ saw the artillery and scampered up the stairs for the roof. The man looked fevered—like he had more than arrests in mind—and JJ didn't want to test the vengeance of authority.

Someone—maybe the new Triad worker—pulled iron, and all hell broke loose promptly. JJ pulled his Raven and emptied it, firing down into the moving shadows. The heat opened up their .38s, returning fire. The shotgun went off. The new bagman fell, gushing blood from his chest and mouth.

JJ stumbled over him and continued up. He made the roof, leaped to the next building, then the next.

They were close, bullets whizzing around his head. He ducked in and put a fresh clip in his iron, quickly emptying it and booking.

Below, on the street, sirens wailed and patrol cars blinked and darted frantically. A Black Maria sat mid-block, loading up with chains of lost souls. An ambulance screeched to a halt. Gunfire punctuating screams of exploding chaos.

Something moved behind JJ, and he spun and fired.

A shadow bit the tar. But he'd given away his position and was drawing fire from two points. No sense dropping it now. They'd kill him for sure. He took off again, miraculously made the next roof. He hurdled a ledge and fell one story to the next building.

It was a brick skeleton JJ used to work, and he knew something about it that just might save his life. It was one of the few constructions on the Lower East Side that had a sub-basement. A trapdoor in the basement led to a stairway, which led to a dank, damp, forbiddingly slimy pit. Beyond this small room was a narrow tunnel, possibly a sewer line.

JJ stormed down the stairway a landing at a leap, smashing into the wall facing the stairs each time. He made the basement, then the subcellar.

Sweat burned his eyes as pain attacked his chest and sides. Adrenaline pumped through him as he flew through the putrid cellar into the darker tunnel. Cool slimy water soothed his swollen agonized ankles. Sparking a lighter after crawling twenty feet, he shivered in horror. A decomposing, half-eaten corpse stared dumbly at him from a corner. Rats scurried off to avoid the intruder, and a spoon and weeper fell. It'd been the dead man's gimmicks.

The tunnel opened onto a damp stone room with all the charm of an abandoned vomitorium. Nothing living had been in this place for a long time, except rats. There was a ledge above his head, and he went for it. He slipped on slimy surface, falling and getting a taste of heinous water in his mouth. On the second try he made the ledge.

JJ chased the rats away with a stick, then lay back using his denim jacket as a pillow. He lit a cigarette. Every bone burned. He had a bundle on him, in a waterproof box. It was dry. JJ placed the iron where he could get to it in a flash. He quickly opened two bags and prepared gimmicks. Both ankles were sprained, getting swollen, and he was scraped bad, in some spots to the bone.

Have to sit tight. They will kill me. No food. No water. Pack of butts and my bags. One more clip left. Six rounds.

After a while he began to nod, but a few hungry rats woke him by going for his ear. Ugly bastards. He'd have to stay awake. He fought the nod until time made him straight.

Hours of detached vacant agony . . .

Gradually he stopped smelling the rancid effluvium, slowly assimilating it. Suddenly, inexplicably, he burst into tears. *"His soul had approached that region where dwell the vast hosts of THE DEAD."* In the dripping shadows a dark, impalpable form . . . Furman D. Whittle? . . . quivering in agony dripping hot wax powdered onto his blinded eyes wishing for death to swing down low on the sweet chariot of a merciful hotshot. "I wanna go somewhere it don' hurt no mo'." Eight bags left. Enough for uno adios. "See here, m'main, le's not go'n git all existential, it jus' give you warts." Self-mocking laughter in the coal bin prop the corpse into comfortable positions. Above the sirens wail. Messy business.

"Furman! Z'at you?"

"Shit be strong, JJ. Eight left. *Make yo' play*. Got a gimmick?"

"Yeah . . . I got a gimmick."

"What ch'waitin' on, m'main? *Make yo' play!*"

JJ threw eight bags in the cooker. Death soup. He drew it up into the chamber. Smokin' poppa! He looked at the point of the weeper. He'd seen plenty of points in his day, but knowing where this one was going made him stare at it. He hit a line.

The eyelids descended in a final curtain.

Nightfire

Police sweeping out the Lower East Side heroin emporium did not wipe Tommy out . . . completely. It cost him plenty. It was apparent that the primary focus of the police blitz was Triad. They were hit with all the ferocity of an urban swat team in frontal assault. Rodent scraggly junkies with snot dangling from torn coats suddenly whipped out badges and guns, rematerializing as undercover narcs. Plainclothes burst out of Con Ed trucks with guns drawn and arrest reports dangling from their back pockets. Burly dicks oozed out of taxis, laundry trucks, out-of-state cars, after watching or triggering a transaction. Sirens, police whistles, and the metal click of locking handcuffs.

The occupation was complete, and the street became a shadowed tomb. The vibrance of an open market was gone.

Every crew lost heavy on the invasion. Continued police permeation forced the crew owners—used to heavy cash flow—into stepping back.

But Tommy's losses were, well, to him somehow more personal. His mind had always been methodical. Now he was filing, referencing, analyzing bad news so frantically he felt like hitting the cooker . . . just enough to achieve some remnants of detached objectivity and be able to look this mess in the face. Whew! Ugly face. Inverted daydreams.

He stashed the Jaguar on Staten Island and rolled a rented Chevy out onto the open road. Clunky old heap of Detroit iron. Didn't come near his own wheels. But obviously the heat knew a lot about Triad. After the sweep it came out in the papers that stakeout had been planted for months gathering a picture of the narcotics market on the street. They'd pin the Jag. Somehow the cops thought JJ—who was missing—was the main man. Amusing. Police science, T thought. Like the ginzos Uncle Satano did shylock with, cops are procedural, predictable. A tip becomes a lead. The lead becomes a theory. Progressional logic takes over, however flimsy the first premise.

After driving onto the ferry T took out a mirror, a narrow sterling straw, and a small plastic bag of pure goodness. Two snowy lines went up his nose. The ferry ride from Staten Island to Manhattan took just over one-half hour. He set his alarm watch for twenty minutes. That way he'd return to the car and sniff a line of coke so he'd be straight enough to drive off the ferry. Just a brief interlude of reflection.

Tommy took a walk and found a deserted spot lower starboard.

With Alvira gone it all rested on his head. The dope giving him distance, he began the dreaded inventory. He'd just reupped when the shit fell. He lost virtually millions in cash and material. Some of it, most even, was his own. But over three bucks belonged to Unc and his wise guys. Ginzos. They would not be amused, forgiving, understanding. *Pissed* is what they'd be! Pissed and nasty. Well, T did have some assets left, and some material. But he needed cash to bail out men he hadn't gotten to already, before someone sang. So far every Triad arrested had pulled a tight lip. T had to keep up his end of things. His cash stash was almost gone, but he did have dope. The dope was worthless without a crew. He couldn't let the old crew work while out on bail. Too risky. And throwing a new crew together would be all but impossible. Triad had already assimilated the cream of the crop as far as slumbums. Very little worthwhile human material left. Maybe he could off some shit on other retailers, but he'd have to sell wholesale and take losses.

Other retailers! Had ShyWun known about . . . ? Nawww. The throne is on fire! My kingdom for some horse.

He poked on a reefer, watching Manhattan lights get closer as the sun dropped below the horizon. Everything was sure different just a short few weeks ago. Oh, there were problems. Alvira's desertion threw a swamp of business details on him, and petty complications proliferated. But Triad was set up and functioning. Leadership was only necessary to keep things smooth.

All different now. Unfamiliar, fear-inspiring. He'd dumped the downtown cribs and rented new digs on 100th Street and Riverside Drive, looking down on the Hudson River. A nice sunny place. But one with no past, and with none of his boys around to remind him of how essential he was.

JJ was missing and had been since the first day of combat. Chu had blown away an informer and was undercover in Philly chilling out. Muggles made bail and was stashed away with some relatives in Wilmington, Delaware. That fact threw a wrench into the Rasta reefer trade. No cake coming in.

Four crew workers were dead, nine arrested, six on the lam. Two for shooting cops. This was eternal heat. The *14-K* was wiped out before it could bud. In fact the whole upper echelon of Triad—excluding the Emperor—was gone. Whoosh. No more. Regards from Cognito.

Just Tommy left. With no one to acknowledge his masterful position.

For the first time since it happened, T admitted to himself

that maybe it wasn't weakness or stupidity that made Alvira duck out. Walking away from power was incomprehensible to T. Maybe Alvira understood something T didn't.

The alarm watch sounded, summoning him back to consciousness. He jumped. It was uncool to get too far inside himself now. No one to cover his back.

Tommy Sparks was now as vulnerable as the next man.

*

Later, T's head rolled loose and light as the fix hit. He laid back on his couch when the phone sounded.

"Listen, kid, make a move quick. I'm not futzing around, Tommy. If you don't show class I'm a dead man."

T knew Uncle Satano never spoke on the phone. The urgency scared him. He'd never heard fear in Unc's voice before.

"I can throw out half a buck right now, Unc." He would dump material below cost and wipe out his gold coin collection. Dump some valuable jewelry. His Rolex collection. The genuine Tiffany lamps he'd bought when things were looking good.

"Half a buck! We're talking over three bucks! These people are dangerous, T. Even for me. You're going to make sparks, Mr. Sparks!"

"Toss them the half and ask for a little time. Gimme a month to turn some material above wholesale and—"

"Month? We're talkin' days, kid. Look, come drop the half and we'll talk. No, don't come here, for chrissakes."

"I dumped the Jag. Got a rented car—"

"Good. Meet me in Brooklyn. You know that cemetery where your father is buried?"

"Sure. Caton and McDonald—"

"Right. One hour from now. Be there."

"Unc—"

"How the fuck did I let so much money ride on your wild ideas?"

"Uh, Unc . . . can't you think of a more cheerful spot to—"

Click!

*

The Chevy topped a hill, and Tommy could see a multi-stratified set of dimensions. Directly below was his father's grave, set into imposingly beautiful landscape. The marble structure of the family plot was awe-inspiring. There was a space for him there. His eyes moved up, and he could see beyond the park, across Brooklyn to the water. The breathtaking complexities of the view distracted him until. . . .

The chauffeur-driven Buick pulled up below. Ominous forms moved behind smoked glass. T's eyes took in a place of the dead. His father was dead, and who'd ever had more life than the old man?

Unc's driver got out, checked around until he spotted T, got back inside.

Triad was also dead. Somewhere in the depths of his subconscious this seemed untrue or at least impermanent. No matter how shitty things seemed, at his level recovery was possible. He was Tommy Sparks!

But for now, best act on the tip it's dead. His brainchild. No funerals. Just a fade, like when a day is over. The sun has set. The day is gone . . . like Furman D. Whittle. Once he liked Furman, but that part of Tommy was long dead as well.

He was in silent harmony with the rows of graves.

They spoke briefly in the back of the Buick. Tommy dropped his half-buck, stacked out neat in an attaché case on the seat. He promised more soon.

"They have to show class, too, Unc." T looked down. "They all know shit fell on me."

"They're afraid you'll pack it in or get killed. Then what?"

"I'll be cool."

"Or get busted. I don't know about you, Tommy. You had to run it to the ground. You could've done it a little less formal, you know, where you're on and off with material. Work a week, skip a month. Guys get rich doin' that, and the cops are always lookin' for the other crews, the ones that keep it up steady. Why'd you have to set up ongoing and permanent?"

"Worked a long time, Unc. How many times I double cake for you and your bozos?"

"Don't be cute, Tommy. There's no play here. Cool the debt in forty-eight hours or we're both dead men. I'll help if you can't pull it. Only way to keep either of us alive. But I can't turn up cash like that without some frantic inconveniences, to say the least."

"Then let's split, Unc. Let's take what we got and pull out! We could live a lifetime on combined cash." He pointed to the attaché case.

Uncle Satano's eyes bulged in anger and outrage at the suggestion. Tommy didn't have to be told it was unthinkable to walk away from the power and position of one's own empire. even if things did turn around. Was it stubbornness, pride, ego? Uncle Satano had killed to etch himself a place in the moneylending game. He'd done time, bought and sold connections, favors, cops, judges and juries, businesses and people. He had been—until this unfortunate incident—a major force in his circle of dons. No walking away from that. Forget it.

"Break cupcakes, kid. But take care of it. Get up that cake. We have forty-eight hours. Call me every three or four hours. Goodbye for now."

The driver's thick form appeared outside the car, opened it for Tommy. Nothing else left to say but . . .

"Unc—"

"Just get it up . . . or we die!"

He got it up. Most of it, anyway. Uncle Satano laid out half a buck, and T got the rest. His thank-you was:

"Good luck, kid. I don't wanna see you for a while. Almos' gave me a fuckin' heart attack. You really set me back

143

with my people, Tommy. We're paid off and clean, and you don't owe me nothin'. Get lost . . . right?"

"Right."

T watched his uncle get into the rear of the Buick. It drove off. He stood by his father's grave for a few minutes, then looked up at an angry sky.

He felt clean. He'd bailed out all his boys and advanced good lawyers a set sum to keep them all out of the can. That took most of his cash and personal possessions. To raise cake for Unc he had to dump all his heroin below cost to the few dealers who'd go near him. Most considered him too hot to touch.

He had three grand and an ounce of cut commercial heroin to his name. The Jaguar would bring in another few grand. But he still had debts and his resources would not come near the final number.

He stood over the family plot and hoofed a large pile of powder off a hand mirror. Next to his parents' grave sat space for his own. He stared at it a long time. Well, is it *no, not yet, I have things to do*? Or is it *yes, I'm ready*? Be so easy to do a few more snorts and just lie back on the grave. Be a warm soft pleasant death. No more problems or loose ends to torment over.

But wait! Not time! Whew! Of course not! He was *still* Tommy Sparks!

That afternoon Tommy returned the rented Chevy and took a modest crib in Brooklyn. The obscurity of Bay Ridge would cover him for now.

∗

Wind blew fiercely through arteries and conduits of junk turf. There was ice on the street. On Eldridge and Houston a bright nightfire burned from the heart of an old oil drum, a crew of lotus ghosts shivering around it as they waited for customers to relieve them of their day's material.

"Dr. Nova is smokin', poppa!"

"The Doctor is in!"

"Fan out yo' cake!"

T stepped up just as a line was forming and had to wait his turn. The guy before him bought two bundles and cleaned out the bagman. Tommy waited ten minutes in the cold while the crew boss sent a runner to reup. He shivered, cold and junk-sick, praying he'd score before the police came.

Word was Nova was the smoker lately. Somehow ShyWun had survived the sweep. Others too. Who knew how or why? Since he lacked capital and credit, there were no lines of communication open between Tommy and ShyWun.

"Four," he said as the bagman opened a fresh package.

T dropped his last forty bucks into the counter's hand and scooped up his bags. He had just enough change for a subway back to Brooklyn. That left no cash for morning.

Alone in the dark stillness of his dim Brooklyn crib, T clamped and unclamped his fist until the mainline stood out like a purple rope. He booted two bags. Already some scar tissue was forming. No need to be discreet. For the moment he could track his arms all he wished.

The Emperor's eyelids descended calmly as he felt the lotus soothe his ravaged mind. "Heavy blood in you," Alvira once said. "Got to live up to your father and uncle. Me, I have nothing to live up to. I'm free." A smile crept onto T's lips. Alvira, as an infant, had been found in a garbage can in an alley behind Alvarado Street in L.A. The Mexican woman who discovered him sold him to a family of New York Jews.

Tommy prepared a backup shot out of the other two bags. He tapped the air out of the cylinder, capped the tip of the weeper, placed it carefully on the bed next to him.

Maybe one day he'd see Alvira again. Maybe one day he'd be with people who knew who he was.

Glossary

This glossary is written with the ear and is entirely phonetic.

Agua	(Spanish) police
B	brother; bro'
Babanya	(Italian) heroin
Bad company	informer or undercover
Ba hondo	(Spanish) police
Bean	brother; bro'
Blanco	(Spanish) white
Bleed	nonblack
Blood	black
Bundle	ten dime bags
Burn	beat for money; a tattoo
Button	made man
Cake	cash
Chill out	detox; calm down
Chinaman	opium
Chinga	(Spanish) sexual intercourse
Cooker	bottle cap; spoon to cook fix

Cool	no sense talkin' about this word
Cop	to score; police
Cura	(Spanish) fix of heroin given to crew workers
De nada	(Spanish) thanks
Dinero	(Spanish) money
Dope	heroin
Double D	strong heroin
Downtown	heroin
Dread	(Rasta) dreadlocks
Drop a dime	inform; make a phone call
Ease off	taper dosage down gradually
Embalao	(Spanish) hopelessly addicted
Esta bien	(Spanish) all clear
Fao	(Spanish) detective (literally, *ugly*)
Fows an' bows	blow harmonies
Ganja	(Rasta) marijuana
Gimmick	hypodermic
God's own	heroin
Goodness	heroin
Gram	one twenty-eighth of an ounce
Heat	police
Heroin	God's own
High	stoned on God's own Rx
Holdin'	heroin on person
Hole	hole in boarded-up building to pass cake in and dope out
Iron	pistol; motorcycle or car
Jesus jizz	methadone
Joint	marijuana cigarette; prison
Jones	dope habit
Junk	heroin
La hara	(Spanish) police
Long	big American car
Marimay	(Romany) dirty informer; person to avoid
Material	what crew workers and bosses call heroin
Maytagging	cleaning money

Membrane	unhip person
Mometta	(Spanish) hot female
O	opium
Off	not using, clean
On	using, high
On the money	quality heroin worth the price
Pick up	score
Play	extra bag for buying bundle
Poppa	what touters call customers
Program	methadone program
Reefer	marijuana cigarette
Schmeck	(Yiddish) heroin
Schmooz	heroin
Score	cop heroin
Short	small foreign sports car
Sick	junk withdrawal symptoms appearing
Smokin'	high-quality heroin
Sound on	suggest
Spliff	(Rasta) thick joint of marijuana
Taken off	robbed
Tapped out	no money
Taxed	robbed
Tecata	(Spanish) heroin
Tip your mitt	reveal
Ven acá	(Spanish) come with me
Vendador	(Spanish) heroin dealer
Vig	loan shark's interest rate
Weeper	hypodermic syringe (usually number twenty-five)
Yen	need for heroin

Crew Hierarchy

Crew boss	Holds money. Serves as bank. Directs workers. Calls all shots on the street. A boss will split every hour or so to deposit money and pick up material.
Moneyman	Takes and counts cash. Passes it on to the bank or boss, counted and with bills facing same way. Will not take singles.
Bagman	Holds bags and makes actual pass. Will not take cash. (No marked money on him.) The bagman takes most direct risk.
Stashman	Feeds bagman. Hides and reclaims packages: small brown paper bags containing fifty-four dime bags (five bundles, four extra for play).
Protectors	Armed and mean backup lurking around to protect crew (and customers because muggings are bad for business.) Protectors earn $200 daily just hanging around, as no one in their right mind would take off an organized crew.

Steerers	Hawk a brand name and lead or point you to it (tip you to it).
Touters	Same as steerers.
Lookouts	Outer perimeters of a crew's op. Far corners, rooftops, points of usual police entry into junk turf. Lookouts' whistles and cries of "Ba hondo" (police), "Fao" (detectives), and "Esta bien" (all clear) ring through the street like a frantic, lyrical calypso spirit.

(This structure is by no means a rule but represents a highly evolved professional op in midregime.)